Pack of Lies

The Twenty-Sided Sorceress: Book Three

Annie Bellet

If you want to be notified when Annie Bellet's next novel is released and get free stories and occasional other goodies, please sign up for her mailing list by going to: http://tinyurl.com/anniebellet. Your email address will never be shared and you can unsubscribe at any time.

This book is dedicated to Demon Fox:
Curse you for all the total party kills, and all the
unskippable cut scenes.

Four pairs of eyes watched the twenty-sided die bounce across the hex mat, life and death riding on its little blue plastic numbers. We had gathered in the back room of my game shop for our usual Thursday night game session. First one since I'd returned from Three Feathers. Steve hadn't been able to make it, but the twins were here, and Harper of course. She'd stood by me while I moped and struggled to resume training to fight my psychotic ex-lover.

While I pined for my other probably ex-lover. Who hadn't called me in over a month. The leaves were going to start changing. Our summer together, the ending of it in total disaster, it seemed like a weird dream now. I missed Alek like hell, but I was recovering. Sorta.

Okay, I'd admit it. I'd been a mess. It felt good to game again, to resume some semblance of normal life again.

"Nat TWENTY," Ezee yelled as the die finished its roll and sat in the middle of a knocked-over pile of orc miniatures. The coyote shifter flipped his thick black hair back from his forehead and pumped a fist in the air.

"All right," I said, hiding my grin. "You successfully perform the heal check. Harper, err, I mean Liandress the Unlucky, stabilizes."

"Cheap bastard," Harper muttered. "You could have just given me a potion."

"Potions are reserved for people who don't cast fireball in small rooms," Levi said, reaching over and ruffling Harper's hair. She flicked one of his many facial piercings, sending the dangling seashell shape hanging off his lower lip spinning.

"What are you doing next?" I asked, before this could end in Harper or Levi flipping the table or tearing out piercings.

"I'll waste a heal spell on this useless wizard here," Ezee said.

"I'll loot the bodies," Levi added. He winked at me, leaned away from Harper, and slid a note across the table.

"Not the notes again," his twin groaned.

Harper rolled her eyes.

I had to admit, as I watched my friends bicker, that it was good to be here, to be doing things with them again. I felt like I was coming out of a fog, finally. For a week after I had returned from Three Feathers, after my anger and arrogance had gotten my father killed, I'd been despondent. Samir's games had gotten to me. Had nearly killed my tribe, killed my whole family, such as they were.

I'd stopped the killings, true. But I'd gotten the man who I had thought was my father killed in the process. I had been banished from my childhood home a second time. That part stung less than knowing that Samir had manipulated me, tricked me. I felt like his little puppet toy on a string, dancing until he got tired and smashed me.

It wasn't a good feeling. All the training in the world, training to become strong enough that I could fight him head-on, it seemed pointless. He wasn't facing me head-on. Instead he kept up his little postcards.

Alek had heard me out, heard the whole story of Shishishiel and Not Afraid, heard how I freed the spirit or whatever it was and saved everyone, though at a cost. He seemed to understand. He told me it wasn't my fault, that my only mistake had been acting so quickly, and acting alone.

I was used to working alone, being alone. This whole having friends who knew who I was and the dangers that posed and who didn't care was a new thing. The whole idea of having a relationship with someone was a new thing.

A thing I apparently sucked at.

Alek and I had talked a little, but I hadn't been ready for more, not right after. I'd retreated, hiding from everyone, alone in my grief and my pain.

Then Alek left. Justice business, he said.

He didn't call. He didn't come back.

I didn't quite pull a Bella from *Twilight* and mope for weeks, but it was a close thing. Harper kicked my ass out of bed after a week of me pretending I didn't need to eat or bathe, and made me come run the store.

"Life gives you lemons, you poke it in the eye with a stick," she'd said.

"Fuck you," I'd said. "I am just making a mess of everything."

"So he's gone. Either suck it up and call his ass, or stop moping."

"It isn't just Alek," I had muttered. "I don't know how to stop Samir. I hate this waiting."

"So get out of bed and train."

"It's that easy?"

"No. It's hard. But you gotta get up and do it anyway." She had settled down on the bed beside me and tugged on my admittedly greasy black braid. "I'm a professional gamer. And a woman. You know what that's like? I get told I'm gonna get raped, that I'm ruining the game, that I should go back to playing with Barbies, that my hair is too masculine or that my boobs are too big or small or whatever, and all kinds of stupid shit. All the time. It sucks. But I don't let it break me and I don't let it stop me from doing what I love, from being who I am."

I knew some of the things people said online to and about her. I'd seen the comments, read the tweets. She never seemed bothered by it. I realized I'd just assumed she wasn't and hadn't ever asked. Great, on top of everything, I was a shitty friend, too.

"How do you do that?" I asked, resolving in my head to ask my friends more about their lives. Be more involved. They were risking everything by wanting me to stay in Wylde, by helping me train. Maybe it was time I started risking my heart for them.

"I tell myself every morning that today, today I'm going to kick ass and take screenshots." And with another tug on my braid and a bright grin, she had leapt up and started raiding my closet.

5

Kick ass. Take screenshots.

I wanted to screenshot this moment, my three best friends gathered around a table in a comic book and game store that I owned. Nobody trying to kill me. Just people who cared that I was here, people who I would die to protect. This was happiness.

"Okay," I said. "You walk down the long hallway and see a set of huge doors. They open as you draw near, as though inviting you inside. The room is circular, with an ornate ivory throne sitting on a dais at its center. A man in red robes rises and greets you each by name."

"I ready my crossbow," Levi said.

"I've got the fireball wand online," Harper said.

I reached into the messenger bag at my feet and drew out a flashlight. I clicked it on and pointed it at the ceiling. The words "unskippable cut scene" were illuminated instantly.

"Woah. How long did that take you?" Ezee asked.

"Not that long," I lied. It had taken most of a season of *Highlander* while I wrestled with the stupid idea, trying to get the words to project properly.

Ezee, Levi, and Harper all swiveled their heads at the same time, just before a knock came on the back door.

"Pizza break! I'll get it." Harper jumped up.

So much for my big dramatic moment where I introduced them to the big bad who would hopefully become their nemesis throughout the rest of the campaign. Gamers. Universe save me.

Joel, the pizza delivery guy, came in and set the pizza warming case down on the side table next to the half-size fridge I keep in here. He was a wolf shifter, one of the few who lived in town instead of out at the official pack home; a giant faux-castle estate that pretended it was a hunting lodge.

"You guys sounded slammed," I said as he pulled the two pizzas from the case, pepperoni and pineapple for Harper and I, everything under the sun plus mushrooms for the twins.

"It's the wake, for Wulf. Every alpha in the States is here, with their seconds." He sighed, rubbing a hand over his short brown hair.

Harper had explained that Wulf was the local pack alpha, a legend. I'd seen him once or twice in town, an old man with white hair and watery grey eyes. His last name was Leifson, supposedly the son of Leif Erikson, the famous Viking who discovered Vinland and the new world. Harper wasn't sure about that, but he was old even for a shifter, over a thousand if the legend was true.

He had died a week ago. Wolf shifters from all over the States were trickling into our small town, causing a weird end-of-summer boom in the hotel and restaurant industry. The hunters weren't here yet, as only wolf season had started and hunting wolves was banned in this county, and the students up at Juniper College wouldn't be back for two weeks, so the business was nice. Not that it was much business for me. Apparently not a lot of gamers in the alpha wolf gene pool.

"They're going to hold the wake on Sunday, right?" Harper said, handing Joel a can of Mountain Dew.

He cracked the lid and drank deeply. "Yeah. Not that non-wolves are supposed to know, you know. Geez guys. Jade isn't even a shifter."

"Small town," Ezee said. "Can't keep anything secret here."

Except me being a sorceress. That was still mostly a secret. Everyone thought I was just a witch. Totally fine by me. Most people, my friends excepted, think sorcerers are evil.

Which might be true. I knew Samir was evil. Me? I wasn't so sure yet. Given how things had gone lately, I figured I could go either way.

I shoved that depressing thought aside. "Well, I wish they'd buy more comic books," I said, smiling.

"They still planning to fight it out for who gets to be the next alpha of alphas?" Ezee asked. Wolf shifters had a weird society, from what Harper and the twins had explained to me. They put a lot of importance and power into their alphas, with everything being run like a gang more or less. Not a thing I was a fan of, after how I'd grown up in a cult and all. Alpha shifters were just shifters who were much stronger than other shifters, sometimes with extra powers. Like Alek, though some of his powers came from him being a Justice and were given to him by the Council of Nine, the shifters' equivalent of a ruling body or gods or whatever.

"Guess so. Glad I'm not an alpha. They are supposed to reaffirm the Peace, too, which I suppose is the real point. I'm keeping out of it. I just deliver pizza, man, and sometimes howl at the moon." Joel laughed, finished his drink, and left with a hefty tip in his back pocket. I'd delivered pizzas for a while, during one of my lives while on the run from Samir. I always tipped well after being in the trenches of pizza service.

We filled paper plates and shoved dice and minis aside to eat. I asked Harper about the Peace, but it was Ezee who answered me, taking on a professorial tone that I knew from his wink was totally an affectation.

"Back in like the eighteen-forties, when everyone was coming west, a lot of wolves from Europe were coming here, making a name for themselves as hunters, trappers, guides, and such. They mixed with the local shifter wolves and formed pretty territorial packs. There was a ton of fighting between packs, enough that it got to the point where humans were starting to notice weird shit like people turning into wolves, and how many people were dying or disappearing."

"Wolves are always territorial. It's like they take the worst traits of wolf and human and combine them into something that resembles neither," Levi said in a tone that made it clear what he thought. His shifter animal was a wolverine, but he was one of the most laid-back guys I knew besides his brother.

"This was bad, though, way way bad. The Council stepped in. Some say that's when they created the Justices as they are today. I don't know. But Wulf, who was still called Ulfr Leifson back then, brought together a huge Althing with an alpha from each of the major packs. To prevent the Justices and the Council from killing them all because they were risking exposure, he brokered a peace. Packs allow all wolves to pass through their territory, and allow non-aligned wolves, like Vivian, or Joel, to live within their territory."

"Like Max," Harper added. Her brother was a wolf shifter as well. He lived with Harper's mom, Rosie, out on a bit of land beyond Wylde, at the edge of the River of No Return Wilderness.

"No fighting, no killing. It saved the wolves from the Council's wrath and kept them from exposing themselves to humans," Ezee said with a shrug. "So now that Wulf is gone, I guess they are going to see who is top dog again and reaffirm the Peace."

"And you think sorcerers are weird? At least we just kill each other," I said with a forced smile. Shifters had seemed so simple. Like people, who could turn into animals. I was learning though, as I slowly paid more attention to the people around me, that they were like any people: far more complex than they first appeared. None of my friends were wolf shifters, so I'd never really asked about packs and politics. Learn something new every day, I guess.

I'd just bitten into my second greasy slice, pineapple juice and spicy pepperoni sliding over my tongue, when a knock came at the back door.

"Probably Joel," Harper said. "Bet he forgot something." She jumped up again and disappeared.

I was halfway through chewing my third bite when she came back, a weird expression on her face as she slid through the door. I swallowed a lump of cheese and started to ask her what was up.

Then I saw the man behind her. Over six and a half feet tall, white-blond hair, ice-blue eyes, and a grim expression on his annoyingly still handsome face.

Alek. And here I was, my hair in a loose braid with pieces falling out, and pizza grease sliding down my chin and staining my teeshirt. Fuck me sideways with a chainsaw.

"Alek," I said, regretting swallowing that last bite so quickly as it lodged in my throat. Or maybe that was my heart, which was trying to punch its way out of my chest in a fight-or-flight simulation.

"Jade," he said, his voice low and soft. He raised one hand, holding up a plastic bag with a wadded-up shirt inside. "I need your help."

The air seemed to go out of the room and I found it hard to breathe for a moment. Anger. Yeah, that's what I was feeling. Hurt and angry.

"Sure," I said. "No problem. Let me drop everything and rush to assist you, Justice. I'll just get my coat." I didn't move.

A glance told me that my three friends were trying their best to turn invisible. Harper pressed herself against the wall to Alek's left, as though her *StarCraft* teeshirt would blend with the *Magic: The Gathering* poster behind her in a sort of nerd wallflower magic. Levi and Ezee, both flamboyant in their own ways, Levi with his Mohawk and tattoos and piercings, Ezee with his silk shirt and pressed trousers, were hunched in their seats, frozen like bunnies sighting the shadow of a hawk. Nobody made eye contact with me.

I guess they would have fled if they could, but Alek's bulk filled the only door.

"Do you know Doreen Reeves?" the bulk in question asked. He didn't seem surprised I wasn't rising to help him despite my words. I guess his lie-detection powers were still intact.

Levi sucked in a breath and then immediately looked like he regretted drawing attention to himself as Alek and I shifted our gazes to him.

"Dorrie. She drives an Explorer," he said with a tiny shrug. "Just fixed her check engine light last week."

"She's missing," Alek said, his cold blue eyes back on my face, turning my skin hot beneath his gaze.

A weird feeling twisted in my gut. "She's a wolf?" I asked, though it was half a question only. Town full of strange wolves. Woman missing. I watched a lot of *Law & Order*, I could do crime victim math.

"Yeah," Levi said. His eyebrows pulled together as though the piercings in them were suddenly magnetized. "Shit."

"Can't your visions tell you where she is?" I said. I was half out of my chair though, holding myself down with an act of stubborn will. I already knew I'd help. I just didn't want Alek to think he could waltz in here after over a month and snap his fingers for his personal sorceress bitch to come magicking for him.

Okay. That was definitely the anger speaking. It left a bitter taste in my mouth that drowned out the pepperoni and pineapple.

"No," Alek said.

I waited, but he didn't say more. Everyone was looking at me. I felt their eyes like physical weights pushing me out of my chair.

"Game's postponed," I said with an exaggerated sigh. "Don't read my notes while I'm gone."

"You do not have to come," Alek said. "Just work spell like you did before, I can do rest." His usually faint Russian accent stood out stronger, and hinted at his own emotions hidden somewhere under his totally stone-faced exterior. I couldn't decide if that made me feel better or worse.

"Nope," I said. "You get me or nothing."

He held out the bag without another word.

I climbed up into Alek's truck and breathed in the scent of hay in sunlight and his own vanilla musk. I'd missed that scent, missed the feel of him near me. It wasn't fair. But I had a job to do. I shoved away my resentment and the mixed emotions of anger and lust and pulled the teeshirt from the bag.

Reaching for my magic, I focused my will into a locate spell, picturing a link between the shirt, which still smelled faintly of sweat and cigarettes, and the woman who owned it, who had, I assumed, worn it last. I'd been training these last few weeks, plus the ordeal in Three Feathers had pushed me to a new level, I guess. I didn't even have to touch my twenty-sided die talisman to work the find person spell. Practice practice practice.

I felt a tenuous link, stretching to the north.

"North," I said. "It's not a strong link."

Alek started up the engine with a nod and drove out of the parking lot, taking the single road out of town, heading north.

"What does 'not strong' mean?" he asked softly after a moment.

"I don't know," I said. "I don't think it's good though. Where did you get her shirt?"

"From her mate."

I risked a glance at him, at his perfect profile in the shifting light from the streetlamps. He didn't elaborate, so I turned my focus back to the spell, to that thin silvery thread only I could see stretching into the darkness.

"You didn't call," I heard myself say.

"We are going to talk now?" Alek said. In the corner of my vision I saw a muscle tick in his cheek. He had stubble, faint and only a shade darker than his white-blond hair. He looked tired, but that might have been a trick of the uneven light.

"No," I said. "Bad timing." I swallowed the "sorry" I wanted to put at the end of that.

After a long moment, he said, "Neither did you."

"Touché," I muttered. Point one to Alek. Great.

The thread of silver veered off to the left, growing thicker as we left Wylde behind. I sat up straighter, peering ahead.

"Left at that turnabout. There's a logging road there, leads to an old quarry. We'll have to park and walk, I think." The quarry was a popular hangout for college students to scratch their names and dirty slogans into the rocks and drink beer and make out. Despite the weak link to Dorrie, this made me hopeful. Maybe Dorrie had run out here with some hot out-of-town wolf to do a little extra-marital mating. Maybe I was about to wreck a marriage instead of find something worse.

There are far more terrible things than a broken relationship.

Alek drove the truck as far down the logging road as we could go, until huge logs dragged there sometime in the past stopped our way. He killed the engine and we climbed out. The air was chillier here than in town, a breeze sighing in the tall trees and sticking my sweaty teeshirt to my back. Summer was definitely over.

I was about to call up a light, which would make holding onto the tracking spell fun, but as I said, practice is practice. Alek beat me to it, pulling a flashlight from under his seat. He shined it ahead of me as I moved carefully down the road and into the quarry.

The hillside here was cut away, a scar on the landscape. Alek's light caught bits and pieces of it as he moved, loose gravel crunching beneath our feet. Darkness pressed in on me. Somewhere, not as distant as I'd have liked—which would have been so far I couldn't hear at all—a wolf howled and was answered by a chorus.

"I've totally seen this movie," I muttered.

"This is the part where we get eaten by a chupacabra," Alek said. He came up close behind me, his muscular body a solid presence at my back. Comforting even as he annoyed me.

His joke made me smile and then get pissed that I was smiling. "Stop being charming," I said, refocusing on the teeshirt in my hands, on the sliver thread of magic pulling me forward into the dark.

"We will talk, Jade," he murmured, his breath warm against my neck, stirring the small hairs there. It sounded like so much more than just a simple promise.

I pushed down the hurt that rose and just nodded curtly, not trusting myself to speak.

We moved slowly through the quarry, the thread growing thicker, pulling me toward where I knew there was a drop-off and a secondary rock fall where they'd mined bigger boulders. We had to be near now.

"Careful," I said. "There's a cliff here somewhere."

After Three Feathers and my out-of-body experience as a woman getting thrown off a cliff to her death by my grandfather, I wasn't overly fond of heights.

"Wait." Alek's hand touched my shoulder as he moved up beside me. He sniffed at the air and made a face. "Blood," he said.

So much for hoping we were going to wreck some love tryst. Why couldn't my life be full of sex instead of violence?

That thought got shoved in the way-way-later file as well. Thinking about sex or violence while standing next to Alek was a supremely bad idea. I'd realized in the last month that I didn't really know this man at all. We'd had a thing, a good thing, I thought. But I knew next to nothing about him other than he was hot, good in bed, a Justice, and would happily watch *Babylon 5* and rub my feet at the same time.

"Old blood?" I asked, but he was already moving ahead, taking the light with him. I stumbled trying to keep up and plowed right into him as he stopped, his flashlight illuminating something blue and black and dead all over. I smelled the death, that horrid scent of drying blood, before my eyes took in the body.

My brain didn't want to make sense of it at first. The blue and black was what was left of the clothing. Blue jeans crusted with blood. Black teeshirt with a Decepticon emblem still emblazoned on it, torn almost beyond recognition. Also covered in blood, and worse. Dried blood covered the stones all around the body. The tiny body. A child.

I lost my grip on the spell and the teeshirt. I sank down to my knees, shaking my head, trying to deny what I was seeing, smelling. Limbs going in directions limbs shouldn't go, attached by what looked like Silly String but was probably strips of flesh. Something had ripped into his belly, and grey intestine bulged out, sharp fecal stench mixing with the sick sweetness of pooled blood.

His face was intact. I knew that face. That face made faces at me, and every other patron of Lansing's Grocery, the only market in town. We all shopped there. Everyone in Wylde pretty much. You had to drive an hour to get to a Walmart, so Lansing's it was.

"Jamie," I said. "That's Jamie." What was he doing out here? No one had reported him missing. He was seven. A little brat of a kid who always hung around the store, cocky and funny. "He likes *Yu-Gi-Oh*. They could order them off the net, but they come to me instead. Every Christmas and his birthday." His birthday was in November. Not so far away.

"Jade," Alek said. He pulled me up and into his arms and I shook there for a moment, weakness winning out. I needed to be held. After a moment I pulled away, not looking at Jamie's body.

"We have to call Sheriff Lee," I said. I patted my pockets, but I'd left my phone charging in the store. Shit. This really was like some stupid horror movie.

"Wait," Alek said. He had turned away from me, sniffing the air, his shoulders tense. He looked more beast than man as he moved off into the darkness.

I picked up the flashlight from where he'd set it on the ground and followed him until I saw what he had scented, not twenty feet farther into the quarry. More bodies, looking like just more rock until I was close.

I forced myself to walk toward them, carefully stepping around drying splashes of blood and bits of gore and bone. Two adults lay sprawled and torn to pieces. I hardly needed to see their faces to know who they were.

Emmaline and Jed Lansing.

"These are that boy's parents. We have to call Lee," I said, stumbling backward, turning away. Too much death. I was so sick of death. I pulled my braid forward and used it to wrap around my mouth and nose, trying to block the stink. It didn't work.

"We need to find Dorrie," Alek said.

Dorrie. I'd forgotten her. Whatever had done this to Jamie and his parents had probably gotten her, too. I didn't bank on finding her alive, not after seeing what lay near my feet.

I walked stiffly back to where Jamie lay and picked up Dorrie's teeshirt. The thread of silver reappeared as I reached for the comforting heat of my magic. I wished I could track whatever or whoever did that to Jamie, could tear into whatever it was and show it that this was my town, my people. I wanted to rip things apart and my rage scared me even as it warmed me and shoved away my nausea.

We found Dorrie, in her wolf form, partially down the steep hillside less than a hundred feet from Jamie. There was no blood on her that I could see. I held the flashlight steady while Alek skidded his way down to her, loose stones bouncing away down into the dark below. He felt for a pulse, but we both knew there wouldn't be one. Then he lifted her easily and carried her back up the nearly vertical slope, acting as though she didn't weigh two hundred pounds. Shifter wolves, like most shifter's animal halves, are much larger than their wild animal counterparts. More like dire wolves.

I was stupidly glad there was no blood other than a bit of dried gore around her mouth. Then that sank in. The torn bits of Jamie, of his parents. Blood on the wolf's mouth.

"How did she die?" I looked at Alek as he set her down carefully outside of the patches of blood and gore staining the area around Jamie's body.

"Looks like a broken neck," he said with a shake of his shaggy blond head. His hair had definitely gotten longer and he didn't have it pulled back in his normal queue.

"That wouldn't kill her, would it?" Shifters healed quickly, almost as quickly as sorcerers from what I knew. Especially if they could just shift, trading their human or animal body for whichever one wasn't injured. Then wherever they went would put them in a kind of stasis, I guess, where they could heal the damage to that body while they ran around in their other one. They were tough to kill what with all the metaphysical body-swapping.

"Not like this," Alek said. "If the connection between body and brain were severed, yes, but this is sloppy. Not even full spinal break. It is lie."

"And the blood around her mouth? Tell me that isn't what I think it is." I pressed my lips into a line and stared earnestly into his face.

23

"It is," he said. "I think those people were killed by wolves. I think we are meant to believe it was this one."

"But?" Please, Universe, let there be a huge-ass *but* attached to the words he was saying.

"It wasn't this wolf. I think she was dead already. There is something, I do not know how to say it, something wrong with her scent. Something tainting her." He raised an eyebrow at me in silent question.

I drew on my magic again, searching the dead wolf's body for signs of magic, signs a spell had been used on her that would either make her kill a child, or kill her while making it look like she'd died falling down a hill.

"Nothing," I said as my magic slid over the dead body with the same reaction it would have had sliding over the boulders around me. "Now can we call Lee?" Sheriff Lee was a shifter, and she was a wolf, but she also had a duty to the human residents of Wylde. Humans like the Lansings had been. This was a crime scene.

Fuck. I swallowed the bile that rose in my throat.

"No," Alek said. "We cannot call police."

"Excuse me," I said, rising to my feet even as he did. "I swear for a moment you said you weren't going to call the police."

"Think, Jade," he said, biting off each word as though they would cut his tongue if he weren't careful. "Little boy and two adults killed by wolves? Here? Now? With the Peace being reaffirmed and every alpha around in town? Your town is crawling in wolves, in shifters. But they won't be able to stop the humans here from going on warpath, from hunting every wolf they find, wild animal or shifter, until they get enough bodies for retribution. And that is not saying what the alphas will do, how they might turn on each other as suspicion grows."

He shifted his weight and looked down at Dorrie's body, her red and brown fur lit up by the abandoned flashlight. "Someone killed her and tried to frame her, a Wylde pack wolf, for these murders. This is Justice work, not human police work."

"The Lansings are human, normals. Besides, Sheriff Lee isn't human; she'll understand the need for silence on aspects of this crime," I said, wrapping my arms across my breasts as the wind picked up. I pretended the shivers I felt were all the breeze and not the chill suddenly clutching at my heart.

"True. But more than local cops will get involved. A child is dead. A whole fucking family is ripped apart out here. This will bring in too much attention, too many complications."

"Alek," I said, but then stopped. I knew what he was proposing. He wasn't going to leave the bodies here, where someone could find them in the next day or so.

This place wasn't exactly deserted, especially on weekends. He was going to hide them, cover up the crime. It might not have been Dorrie who killed Jamie or his parents, but we both knew no wild wolf had done this. "You can't."

"I have to," he said, his voice rough, coming out as more growl than human speech. "Wait in truck if you want."

"No," I shrieked. "No, fuck no. I am not going to let you do this. People are going to notice they are missing. They have friends, family. You going to deny their family closure? Fuck you. I won't let you do this." I shoved him, hard. He didn't even give me the dignity of stepping back.

"I have to," he said again, folding his arms around me. I struggled but the effort was half-assed. "They would have closure, perhaps, but there is too much more death down that path. Death of wolves. Death of innocents. The guilty is a shifter, maybe more than one. You and I know this. The humans aren't equipped to get justice for his family, to stop whoever did this from doing it again. I am." He pressed his lips to my forehead, burning hot against my chilled skin. "This is who I am, kitten. This is what I do."

It was the endearment that broke me. Or maybe his logic. He was right, but I hated him for it.

I refused to help with the bodies, stubbornly sitting in the truck after Alek loaded Dorrie's body into the back and covered her with a tarp. I pretended it was morals instead of cowardice and pain that kept me from helping Alek cover up the murders. A family murdered, three people I saw weekly, people I knew, if not well. A wolf shifter killed also, left nearby in a way where someone clearly intended whoever found Jamie and his parents to think the wolf had killed them.

I pulled up my knees and wrapped my arms around them, staring out the windshield toward where Alek was doing whatever he was doing. This was fucked up. I worried it was Samir; my evil ex reaching out to stir up shit in my life and see what I'd do again. Somehow I didn't think it was, however. This felt too impersonal for Samir. Killing a child, a whole family, I'd totally lay that at his feet. But he couldn't have known that I would be the one to find the bodies. And he would have known I'd never fall for the whole "look over here at this dead wolf that must have broken its neck or been chased off by its pack after eating these people" trick. It was stupidly obvious. Too obvious. Meant for hysterical relatives, perhaps. Law enforcement faced with an angry and grieving community. People who would be looking for the obvious, the easy answers, the easy way to retaliate.

This wasn't Samir. This was something else, someone else. Shifter business. Great.

Of course, I'd been wrong about that before. Recently.

When Alek finally returned to the truck, he was covered in dust and bits of gravel. Grime lined his face like bad makeup, highlighting his cheekbones and the wrinkles in his forehead. He pulled his sweat-soaked shirt off and used the inside of it to wipe his face. He grabbed another shirt from a bag I hadn't noticed stuffed behind the bench seat of his truck. I tried not to watch, but couldn't help myself, grateful for the dim light from the nearly full moon as it crested the trees. Alek climbed in without saying a word to me, started the truck, and backed up down the logging road.

"There will be a huge search when the Lansing family is reported missing," I said after a tense moment.

"Yes," he said. That was it, just *yes*.

"They will look out in the woods. They will check the quarry."

"No one will find their bodies." He said the words as though they were a comment on the weather, but he said them in Russian. Alek sometimes reverted to his native tongue when truly upset. First his accent would get very strong, then English would fail him.

He sounded certain. I let it go, for now. I didn't really want answers. Yet.

When tires hit asphalt, I spoke again.

"I want in. All the way in. No 'Justice business, you shouldn't get involved' bullshit from you. You made me a part of this and I'm going to see it through."

"All right."

I finally turned and looked at him. He glanced at me but his face gave nothing away.

"Good. So it's settled."

"It is," he said in an infuriatingly agreeable tone.

"So where are we going with Dorrie's body?"

"The vet."

"I don't think Dr. Lake's practice is open this late," I said.

"It is now," he said. "I made a call."

Vivian Lake, the town vet, let us in the back. Her office was the bottom part of an old Victorian-style house. The tiny wolf-shifter merely pursed her lips and sighed as Alek preceded us into the house with Dorrie's body over his shoulder. I didn't know what he'd said to her on the phone, but unlike the last time I'd come here asking her for an autopsy, she definitely wasn't surprised.

It was weird déjà vu. Alek and I showing up with a dead shifter was basically how Alek and I had met. Only that time the shifter, Harper's mom Rosie, hadn't been actually dead, just frozen by evil magic and being used as a battery by a warlock.

A trick that technically, since I'd eaten Bernie the bad warlock's heart, I could also do. Not a fun thought. I left

Bernie's memories the hell alone most of the time, not wanting that power. The one time I'd touched them, I'd made a huge mistake and gotten my not-really-my-father killed. Fuck that.

Alek laid Dorrie on the exam table while Vivian pulled on gloves. She glanced at me.

"She's really dead?" she asked.

I didn't blame her for double-checking after what happened last time.

"Yeah," I said. I wanted to say something about the Lansing family, the horror of it all bubbling up inside me, but Alek touched my arm gently and gave me a tiny shake of his head.

Fine. I'd let Vivian do her thing, but I wasn't thrilled with his decisions and I glared at him to let him know that. The sadness that flickered in his eyes before his stony mask came down made me feel slightly guilty. But only slightly.

"Oh, Dorrie," Vivian murmured as she began feeling over the body.

"Did you know her?" Alek asked.

"Yes. I do not run with the pack or live at the Den, but I still attended barbeques. Wulf was a very accepting and open alpha. Those of us who chose to live our lives without being officially in the pack were still always welcome." Her voice was steady, but her eyes blinked rapidly for a moment, as though she were fighting tears. When she looked up at Alek, her cheeks were damp.

"Her neck is broken, but that wouldn't have killed her, not like this. And what is this blood? Did she get a piece of her killer?" Vivian asked.

"What killed her then?" Alek said, ignoring her questions.

Vivian shook her head and got out the scalpels. I excused myself and slipped out of the exam room. I'd seen enough internal organs for the day. Or maybe the year.

I read old *National Geographic*s in the semi-dark waiting room, turning on only a single small desk lamp at the receptionist's, Christie's, desk. Outside headlights came and went and I heard occasional murmurs through the exam room door. An hour passed, maybe a bit more.

Alek opened the door and caught my attention with a small wave. I rose and moved toward him. He stayed in the doorway for a moment, just staring down at me. Then he glanced over his shoulder and moved aside. Vivian had draped Dorrie's body with a blue hospital sheet, like they give you in exam rooms to pretend to cover yourself with. I realized Alek had been hiding whatever was under the sheet from my gaze until the body was covered. Annoyingly protective of my sensibilities, as though he understood I was reaching my limit for the night. Yet that little gesture gave me the serious warm and fuzzies.

Fuck. I still had it bad for this guy.

"Well," I said, not moving.

"She was poisoned," Vivian said. She stripped her gloves off and tossed them into the trash, then rubbed at the lines forming on her forehead. She looked like she wanted to go drink half a bottle of whiskey and cry for days. I didn't blame her.

"Poisoned? How is that possible?" Shifters healed too fast for poisons to work well on them, plus they could just purge their systems by shifting and letting the whole magical place where the alternate body lived do the work. Maybe I'd missed something during my discussions on the subject with Harper.

"The poison isn't something I've ever seen," Vivian said.

"Nor I," Alek added, his own forehead creasing. Tension rolled off him like a scent, a tangible presence that tickled my nose and raised goosebumps on my arms. "The poison incapacitated her, put her out instantly so she couldn't shift to purge it. Then it traveled to her heart and ate its way through the organ, destroying it. It damaged her brain and a lot of other organs as well."

"That's fucking just great," I said. "How did they get it into her?"

"Broke her neck first—I found where it started to heal. Injected her in the chest, I think, while she was incapacitated, waited for the poison to kill her, broke her neck again." Vivian squeezed her eyes shut and leaned against the counter. She looked almost childlike huddled against the tall counters, but the pain in her face was old and very adult.

"So, someone managed to hold down a wolf, break her neck, then inject her with this new super poison that eats heart muscle, then waited…" I paused. "Wait. What do you mean, waited?"

"The poison would take time. Many hours, a day or more if the shifter was particularly strong. Even without being able to shift, her body would have been trying to heal the damage the poison was doing as it worked. It just does too much damage and eventually destroys the heart," Vivan said. "I just hope they injected it close to her heart, so it would work more quickly, so she would suffer less."

"This is not good," I said, mostly to myself. Someone was responsible for this, or more likely, some *ones*, because one person would have to be crazy powerful to subdue a wolf, poison her, then pull off abducting and killing a family. Especially in this small town. People would notice.

How the hell hadn't anyone noticed? The town was full of strangers at the moment, that was true. But still, the Lansings ran the damn store. They were fixtures. Jed was always in and out of the deli, recommending cuts of meat. Emmaline often worked the registers, chatting with people about their day. Jamie liked to sit on the mechanical horse outside and show people the gaps in his mouth from the teeth he'd lost. Why had no one reported them missing?

"Reported who missing?" Vivian said and I realized I'd spoken the last part of my thoughts aloud.

"Jade," Alek said, his tone a warning.

Well, fuck him. Vivian was already elbow deep in this. He could deal.

"The Lansing family," I said.

"They aren't missing," Vivian said, her eyes wide with alarm. "They are at Jed's sister's cabin by Bear Lake. Aren't they?"

I guess that made sense then. They'd gone on vacation, but not gotten very far. I just shook my head, looking up at Alek.

"Vivian," he said, his voice terribly soft. "This stays here. You must not speak of what you've heard or seen tonight. Not until I can investigate. Something awful is happening here, things that could threaten the pack and the Peace. Do you understand?"

She nodded. "I trust you, Justice," she said.

I turned away so my face wouldn't betray my disgust with her compliance. It wasn't fair for me to feel this way. Alek was a Justice. The Council of Nine were like gods to the shifters. She would trust him to handle these terrible crimes just like I guess I would trust the State Police or the FBI to solve a murder.

That thought was slim comfort. I didn't think I'd trust them, either.

Only yourself, my evil brain whispered. *Trust only yourself.*

Fuck that. Look where that had gotten me. Great.

I walked out the back door and breathed in the cool night air, trying to clear my senses of death, my head of its confusion. Alek joined me and stood silently beside me.

"I'm pissed at you," I said.

"I know," he said. "Please, Jade. Trust me on this?"

"For now," I said. "But we need to talk. Like really talk."

"So talk."

"No," I said. He laughed and it made me want to punch him. Or kiss him. I had missed that deep, full-bodied laugh of his.

"If I talk to you now, I'll just end up punching you or saying stupid shit I regret. I'm too mad. So I'm going to walk home and you can come find me tomorrow. Call me if you figure out anything else." *Or if anyone else dies*, but I didn't add that last part aloud. It would have felt too much like a prediction.

I didn't wait to see his expression or his response; I just started walking, afraid if I waited, if he said something, somehow the right thing like he usually did, I wouldn't be able to hang onto the burning anger inside of me.

He didn't come after me or call out, just let me walk away. I guess some things don't change.

My store, Pwned Comics and Games, is sandwiched in a rectangular building between two other shops. On one side is my friend Ciaran's pawn shop, a place full of crazy art, antique everything, and a few small, actually magical items. Ciaran is a leprechaun and has a serious case of desire for shinies. He also makes a mean cup of tea.

On the other side of my shop is Brie's Bakery. Brie is some kind of magic user, though I'd never asked her what exactly. It isn't the kind of thing that comes up in small talk, even in a town as full of supernaturals as Wylde is.

My guess was that she's some kind of hearth witch; her magic seemed centered on hearth and home and making people feel good through excellent cooking. I could sense a touch of magic in every bite of every baked good I'd ever eaten from her bakery, but it was the kind of magic you don't mind. Little things, touches of charms to make you feel good, to improve taste and flakiness. Her baking was literally magical.

I hadn't told my friends that, of course. I figured they knew Brie wasn't fully human, since shifters have a good nose for such things, but her secrets, like mine, were her own.

I left Harper in charge of the shop on Friday morning and ducked next door to the bakery to pick up honey scones and two tall teas to go. Ezee was due any minute to take me over to the college and sneak me into the indoor pool there so I could keep working on my training. With the students still gone, the college was almost deserted, and the time of year too late for many people to be using the pool, indoor or not.

The bakery had a decent crowd for a Friday morning. I recognized a couple of locals, but the others were likely visiting wolves. Even predators appreciate a perfect croissant. Brie was behind the counter handling orders herself this morning, a tall woman with fire-engine-red hair in thick curls piled on her head that would make for great Disney's *Brave* cosplay, and an apron that said "Save the unicorns" on it. I greeted Brie with a wave and got into line.

A stocky woman about my height, with reddish-brown hair in a pony tail and a flannel shirt on, was ahead of me, speaking her order in an impatient, brusque tone that annoyed me. Brie was handling her fine, however, so I just glared at the back of the stranger's head and stuck my tongue out a little. I know Brie caught that, because she smiled extra-wide as she handed the woman her order.

The stranger turned quickly and nearly collided with me.

"Excuse me," she said in a tone that said I was the one at fault. Her eyes were dark blue and there was something sharp and almost feral about her face.

I stepped back and started to murmur some meaningless apology when I caught the glint of silver around her neck. Her shirt was partially unbuttoned and a silver feather hung there on a chain. A necklace almost identical to Alek's.

Not that there aren't tons of feather necklaces in the world. But something about her reaction to me looking at it confirmed it. Her eyes widened and she sniffed at me.

"Who are you?" she asked. "You from the rez?"

Yeah, because all us Indians live on reservations. Right.

"Um, excuse me?" I said, dropping any pretense of being polite. "Do I know you?"

"Apparently you do," she said, her already thin lips turning into a white line as she mashed them together.

"I'm just here for delicious baked goods, lady," I said.

She looked me up and down, as though measuring me for my coffin, and leaned in, sniffing at me in a prolonged, obvious way. I became aware of everyone in the bakery now watching us, the strangers and the locals all taking in this woman acting weird toward the comic book lady.

"We'll see," she said. Then she stepped around me and walked out of the bakery.

The tension slid out the door with her and the people parked around the tiny café tables went back to their conversations.

"Lot of strangers in town," Brie said with a smile as she readied my order.

"Yeah, guess so." I wondered if she knew about Justices and the Council. I had a feeling she did.

"Be safe," she said as I juggled my order and my change.

Yeah, she knew. I got that feeling.

So, two Justices in town. I wondered if Alek knew about her. The questions I had for him were piling up. There was a shitstorm building out there with this Peace, these wolves. I felt it in my bones. For a moment I wanted to jam it all into the not-my-problem file, stick my head in the sand and pretend the only thing I needed to worry about was Samir and training to be strong enough to kick his ass back to the Stone Age whenever he finally showed his face.

I couldn't solve everyone's problems. I couldn't even solve my own. So I watched down the street for a moment in the direction the female Justice had gone, pushed away the thought of the Lansing family buried somewhere out there among rocks and silence, said *fuck it* in my head, and climbed into Ezee's car when he pulled up. Time to eat honey scones and then practice breathing underwater.

Everything else would just have to wait.

This was my third session in the pool. The first time had been a total fail, with some hilarious in retrospect almost-suffocation. Nothing like trying to figure out a water-breathing spell and accidentally making it so you can't breathe air normally anymore.

I was better now. Magic for sorcerers is something we are, not just something we do. Unlike a witch or warlock or other human spell-user, we own the raw power—we *are* the raw power. Which meant if I could conceive of it and channel enough power into it, whatever *it* was, I could make it happen.

The mental game was the issue. We're raised with laws. Laws of physics. Laws of nature. Laws about how we can move, what we can do, say, act. Some of these things are flimsy, like human laws about not killing or cheating on your wife or whatever. Some things, like the law of gravity, are pretty strong and without some kind of other force acting on them can't be broken by just anyone.

I can break the rules, but only if I can convince myself I can and summon enough power to do so. That's where my upbringing as a teen with the role-playing game Dungeons & Dragons had come in handy. As I came into my power, my adoptive family had used the only things available to make sense of what I could do, the only real manual we knew of that talked about magic. DnD is fake, of course. It's a game, like many I love and play. In the hands of most people, the spells contained in it are useless. You got to have magic to make magic.

I *am* magic. It's like an extra muscle only I, and others like me, are born with. The more I work with it, use it, the stronger I become.

Which is why I was spending my Friday morning sitting at the bottom of the Juniper College pool, my hair tucked uncomfortably into a swim cap, breathing chlorinated water like it was air, and practicing turning the top of the pool into ice lances and melting them again. Keeping the water-breathing spell and the ice spells going at the same time felt good—a challenge, but not as bad as it had been last week. I was making progress. How this would help against Samir, I had no idea, but I figured the more power I used, the more control I developed, the better.

The trick hadn't been figuring out how to breathe in water. That proved pretty simple, just an act of channeling the power into my lungs, bringing my will in line with the magic. It's magic, after all. It's supposed to do crazy shit without scientific, detailed explanations. No, the real issue had been convincing my body that breathing in water wasn't the worst idea ever. Biological conditioning of tens of thousands of years of evolution said that human lungs breathing in water was a terrible idea. Once I convinced my body that it wasn't going to die horribly, once I forced myself to take that first awful, scary, wet breath, it got a lot easier.

Morpheus was totally right. *There is no spoon.*

I was feeling pleased with myself until a twelve-foot white tiger dropped into the pool. He splashed heavily into the water and swam down, staring at me with open eyes and his nostrils pinched shut like a seal's. I would have freaked out more, but I recognized Alek's tiger form.

With as much dignity as I could summon while sitting at the bottom of a pool in a swimsuit and cap, I let myself rise to the surface, clearing the water from my lungs before I transitioned out of the spell and back to breathing air. Reluctantly I let go of my magic and climbed out onto the side of the pool.

Tiger-Alek leapt out of the water and shook himself before shifting in less than a blink back to his human form. He wasn't even damp, his blond hair loose and fluffy, his black sweater and cargo pants clean and dry.

"I could have accidentally speared you with ice," I said, glaring to make sure he knew I was still mad.

"I'd live," he said with a shrug.

"Ezee still out there? He just let you in, didn't he?" I grabbed my towel from off the bleachers and wrapped it around myself, aware of how nearly naked I was.

"Yes," Alek said. "He wisely did not argue."

He's a shifter, I wanted to say. *He wouldn't argue with a Justice anyway.* Those words sounded petty to me, and I held them back. Looking around, I noticed a silvery shimmer on the walls. Alek was shielding the room, so at least Ezee wouldn't be able to eavesdrop on whatever we said to each other. Small blessings.

I pulled on a green thermal long-sleeved teeshirt over my damp suit and then struggled into my jeans. I didn't want to talk to Alek without a proper amount of clothing on. I couldn't trust my hormones around him and we really needed to figure shit out before we just jumped back into bed.

If we jumped into bed again. My libido was making a lot of assumptions.

"Is Wolf here?" Alek asked, moving over to sit beside me on the bleachers.

He was talking about my spirit protector, one of the Undying, a guardian of the old gods. I had named her Wolf when I was four after she showed up and carried me to safety out of a mineshaft where my cousins had abandoned me.

"She's around," I said. She was usually around, though I couldn't see her at the moment. In the days following the disaster at Three Feathers, I'd worried that Wolf would abandon me, but she hadn't. As I'd lain in bed despondent and unhappy, she'd crashed on the floor, a huge black presence that occasionally sighed and looked at me with eyes full of stars. She'd disappeared about an hour before Harper showed up, gave me the pep talk, and dragged me out of bed. I hadn't asked Harper, but I had a feeling that Wolf might have fetched her.

Alek just nodded, not explaining why he had even asked. I pulled my swim cap off, shook out my hair, and moved into a cross-legged position facing him. I snagged a braid tie from my pocket and started finger-combing and braiding my waist-length hair into some semblance of order.

"So," I said. "You didn't call."

"So," he said. "You didn't call."

We both cracked weak smiles. I started to speak but he reached out with one hand, as though to touch my cheek, but he stopped short and withdrew it, curling his fingers into a fist in his lap.

"I do not like being away from you," he said. I raised an eyebrow at that but let him go on. "I have been with women before but never for long. Always, I had to leave. I am a Justice first. I cannot let attachments to people or place interfere." His tone implied old hurt, old pains. I wondered who else, or where else, he'd left that he regretted.

"Did I ask you to stay? Did I ever tell you not to do your job?" I asked, unable to stay silent.

"You did last night," he said.

"That's isn't fair, Alek. You covered up a crime. You basically said that the potential death of a shifter is more important than the actual pain and suffering of a human family."

"Because it is," he said, his voice so soft it was nearly lost in the plink and shush of water in the pool. "I am a Justice. This is what I do, who I am. I serve the Council. I protect shifters. I keep them safe, alive, hidden. Unless they cross the line. Then I kill them." His eyes were hard chips of blue ice, his mouth tight and drawn as he stared at me. "Last night, those bodies, the death. It shocked you. Upset you, no?"

I nodded, not trusting my voice.

"It doesn't upset me anymore," he said, looking away from me, eyes fixed on the water. "I saw that dead child and all I can see are problems that require solutions. The need to find the killer is there, yes, but all I see is that I will have to kill again. Take another life for a life, and in the end there will be only death. My job is not a matter of how many die, only a balance of how many I can save."

"That's..." I said, then hesitated. "Awful." It made a strange sense to me and that feeling twisted me up inside. Part of me understood what he meant. Part of me was horrified by this.

He reached into his shirt and fingered the silver feather. "This is the feather of Maat—do you know the legend?"

I nodded. Maat was an Egyptian goddess of justice and truth. Lore had it that when you died your heart was weighed against her ostrich feather. If your heart was lighter than the feather or the scales balanced, you were good and could go on to whatever reward awaited. I'd forgotten what that reward or place was supposed to be.

If you were bad, another god would eat your heart and your soul would be stuck in limbo.

Thinking about it, there were some creepy parallels to sorcerers. I thought about Bernie's memories and power, which I'd gained by eating his heart. Had I consumed his soul? Trapped him in some weird limbo? Ick. Definitely wasn't going to dwell on that right then.

"I look at it," Alek said, still turning the silver talisman over and over in his long fingers. "And I wonder if my heart would balance the scale. Then I look at you, and I wonder if there could be more to life than killing, if I could be both man and Justice." Deep sorrow and confusion lined his face for a moment as he looked up from the feather and met my gaze.

There were things he wasn't telling me, words I could almost hear in between the ones he spoke, but what he had said resonated. I was afraid of the same things. I was used to being alone, to doing what I thought was best for me and me only. Doing whatever I thought would keep me safe from hurt, any kind of hurt. And I worried about killing, worried about how it didn't bother me like I felt it should.

"It wasn't Sky Heart's death that bothers me," I said. "It was the collateral, the mistakes I made." I knew I wasn't explaining my leap in logic and topic well, or really at all, but Alek slid his hands over mine.

"There are many choices we must make," he said. "Things we have to try to balance. You saved them. Without you, many more would have died. Without you, your sister would have been thrown from that cliff by her grandfather, as so many others were before her."

"But better than worst isn't good enough," I said. "Fuck, I'm talking in tongue-twisters. I really wanted to just yell at you, you know. I had a speech planned."

"Liar," he murmured, his mouth creeping into a smile as though against his will.

"We're a mess." I turned my hands beneath his, touching his palm to palm. He felt so warm, so alive. Even through the chlorinated vapors coming off the pool, I smelled him—vanilla and that Alek-specific musk that was wild, comforting, and all him.

"I am not good at relationships," he said. "But I want to try. I want to stay, as long as I can."

"I suck at this, too," I said. "I mean, the last guy I was with is currently treating me like his emotional chew toy in prep for smacking me down and nomming my heart."

"I will strive to set a better example," Alek said, his smile stronger, enough so that I could almost forget the deep sadness and confusion he had shown only moments before. Almost.

"Next time, call," I said, squeezing his hands. "Or email. I'm not picky."

"I promise," he said. He leaned forward and brushed his lips over mine. The kiss was a promise too, but it ended quickly, and I bit back a groan. It was good we didn't start making out, I suppose. My mouth still tasted like pool water.

There were so many things that I didn't know yet about him. But maybe this was a real beginning—maybe even someone as fucked up as I was could make a relationship. I guess I shouldn't have expected it to be uncomplicated.

"So," I said after a far too comfortable moment just holding hands and staring at each other. "Where is your gun?" I had noticed he wasn't wearing it the night before, but hadn't had time to ask. It seemed odd to me he wouldn't have it.

"That is a long story," he said, his tone making it clear he had no desire to tell the story at the moment. "I have not replaced it yet."

Hint taken, I changed the topic somewhat. "Any news on the latest psycho killing people in my town?"

"No." The way he said the word made it clear how much that frustrated him. "There are many wolves to talk to, spread out all over. I will go and continue questioning them, but I have to be careful. No one knows yet what has happened and the knowledge getting out in the wrong way could jeopardize the Peace."

"What about the other Justice in town?" I asked. "She know anything?"

Alek's hands tightened on mine and his eyes widened slightly. "Justice?" he said, tipping his head sideways.

"You didn't know." It wasn't a question. It was pretty clear he hadn't. I reached up and brushed a lock of hair from his forehead. "Doesn't your Council tell you guys when they send more than one of you?"

"The Council does not speak to us in so direct a way," Alek said. "What did this Justice look like?"

"Reddish-brown hair, dark blue eyes, about my height, sharp features, and wearing typical hiker gear. Feather around the neck, and a bad attitude. Know her?"

"Eva Phillips," he said, nodding. He didn't look happy about it. "She's a wolf, been around a long time. She was one of the Justices sent to witness the original Peace at Ulfr's Althing."

"I take it you two aren't close?"

"We all mostly work alone. Sometimes, when things are very bad, the Council will send more than one. I have worked with Eva once. It did not suit me. She has no mercy in her."

"It's kind of scary to hear *you* say that, honestly." I rolled my shoulders, thinking of how the woman had looked at me.

"Remember how I thought you were killing shifters? How I listened to you and let you prove you weren't involved?" He rose from the bleachers and paced a little ways down the side of the pool.

"That's sort of how it went, I guess," I said.

Alek turned back to me, his gaze fierce. "If the Council had given Eva that same vision, had sent her, she would have killed you first, asked questions never." The shadows were back in his eyes, worry putting fine lines in his pale skin and turning down the corners of his mouth. His expression sent a shiver down my spine as I sensed that somehow his worry was as much for me as about Eva Phillips. I didn't understand why. More secrets, I guessed. Awesomesauce.

"Fan-fucking-tastic," I said. I pulled my socks on and then strapped on the knife I'd taken from Not Afraid in its ankle sheath before tugging on my shoes. "I guess you should work quickly then, if you can. Question the wolves in town. Want to drop me back at my store?" Part of me wanted to go with him, ask my own questions, see their faces for myself. But Alek was a Justice; they'd talk more readily to him than to him and some random woman who smelled non-human but not shifter. I'd be better later, if someone needed fireballing or protecting or finding. Part of me hoped fireball was the option.

"Great job, Cerberus," I told Ezee as we emerged from the pool.

He gave me a shrug that said it all as he tucked away his Kindle and stood up from where he'd been sitting beside the doors. "You need a ride back?" he said, looking between Alek and I.

"Nah, Alek will drop me off."

"Good," he said, putting emphasis into the word. With an exaggerated wink he brushed off his trousers, picked up his bag, and scrammed like the coward he was. I glared after him, unable to really be mad. A little warning would have been nice, but eh. Friends. What can you do.

Alek held the door for me like a gentleman. I started to walk through, doing the automatic check for keys even though I hadn't driven, and realized that my phone was missing from my jeans pocket. Probably fell out near the pool. I swear that phone was possessed, never around when I needed it. Maybe it knew my rough history with phones. I stopped and turned back.

Which meant that the bullet that should have turned my head into fine pink mist instead cleaved off part of my braid before chunking into the wall and pinning my hair there in an explosion of concrete dust.

Sniper. First thought that went through my head. Watched too many war movies, I suppose. But I wasn't wrong.

I dropped flat as Alek sprang over me. He turned into a tiger in mid-leap and charged the upper parking lot, where the shot likely came from. I blinked dust out of my eyes and squirmed backward into the doorway.

"Alek," I yelled. A car engine roared to life and I heard squeals as it peeled out. Risking a look, I raised my head and crawled forward again, just enough to see up into the lot. The sun was in my eyes but I made out a giant tiger charging after a small SUV. The SUV floored it out of the lot, which fed into the main artery of the school and out onto the highway running away from town. Even Alek couldn't keep up.

He stopped and shook himself, as though only now realizing that he was a twelve-foot-long white tiger standing in an Idaho college parking lot in broad daylight. Then he looked around and turned back to a man in a blink.

I pushed what was left of my hair, which was most of it, thank the universe, out of my face and gathered magic into a shield around me, hardening it to turn away bullets, just in case that car had been a distraction from the real shooter. Then I made myself get to my feet, fighting down the panic. A bullet in the head wouldn't kill me, but I had no idea how long I would take to regenerate from it, and I really, truly didn't want to ever find out. Getting shot hurts like a motherfucker.

I made my way toward the upper lot as Ezee came running back down the hill.

"Was that a gunshot?" he called out.

"Yeah," I said, my ears still buzzing. "I think someone just tried to kill me."

He looked wildly around, sniffing the air.

"They took off in a car," I added. "I think we're okay now."

For now, but how much longer? Pushing that fun thought away, I walked to meet up with Alek, who was standing over something where the car had been parked.

"He left a note," Alek said, crouching down and breathing deeply, mouth half open as though he could taste the air.

A piece of parchment paper lay curled on the asphalt, a single bullet holding it down. There was something written on the paper, brush strokes that looked like Kanji, but I couldn't see enough to make out the word. An odd tingle, a bitter taste of foreign magic like the afterburn of gunpowder on my tongue, warned me just before Alek touched the note.

"Wait," I yelled as I threw my shield bubble around the note, locking it down with as much power as I could pour into it in the fractions of a second before the paper ignited and then exploded.

The blast, even contained within my shield, rocked all three of us off our feet. I fell on my ass, concentrating only on holding all that horrible force inside my magic. Alek and Ezee twisted and rolled, each regaining his feet quickly and gracefully. Damn shifters.

The blast force had nowhere to go but down. The asphalt buckled and split, tar melting and concrete turning to powder. The bullet fired as the force and heat ignited it, shards fragmenting and smashing into my shield, pinpricks of additional force that stung as I wrestled with the blast, holding it down. Inside my body my power waged war against the forces as my bones vibrated and an out-of-tune hum rang in my ears.

Then it was over and the air stilled as though the world held its breath. All I heard was my own coughing breath, my pulse racing. Sweat dripped between my breasts. The jangling feel of my magic stilled in my bones. Slowly I let the shield down. A wave of heat, like standing too close to a bonfire, swept over me, then was gone.

"Fuck," Ezee said. "That was amazing."

"Yeah, that was a hell of an explosion spell," I muttered. I shoved away my bitter memories as they rose—unbidden and unwanted. My second family had died in an explosion. I was not a fan of them.

"No, you," he said, grinning at me with a wild look in his eye. "That would have killed us."

"Not me," I said before I realized how that sounded. I didn't want to think about the fact that my friends, that the man I might be in love with, were a lot less durable than I was. I preferred to think of them as indestructible. I knew in my heart that they weren't. Even I could be killed. But not by a bomb. Or a bullet.

"That shot was at you," Alek said. "Ezekiel left first; it would have been simple to shoot him. Instead, assassin waited until you emerged into light. If you hadn't reversed course like that, poof. No head." His blue eyes were dark with rage. Lucky for the assassin that Alek hadn't caught him. It was cute how protective he looked, how afraid for me he was. Scary, but cute.

"That wouldn't have killed me. Not forever. I'd have grown a new head or something." I waved my hands around to indicate big magic would have happened. I wasn't clear on exactly how much damage I could survive, only that supposedly the single way to kill a true sorcerer is to have another sorcerer eat their heart.

"Then why bother? Unless the killer doesn't know that, I guess," Ezee said.

I shook my head. As the adrenaline left my system, exhaustion set in. I'd slammed a lot of power into that shield and done it quickly. Six months ago we would have all been blown to bits. It was good I'd been training, and a little scary to me how quickly I'd gotten more powerful. Maybe more powerful than I had been when I was with Samir. Sadly, still not powerful enough.

Samir. This had him written all over it. I took a deep breath and struggled to my feet, shaking off Alek's extended hand as he tried to help me.

"I think the idea isn't to kill me, just incapacitate me while he harvests my heart and gives it to Samir." Unless, of course, Samir was here somewhere. Watching.

Waiting. I looked around, trying to pierce the dim treeline, trying to pick out a watcher if there was one. Total paranoia. I wished that thought hadn't occurred to me.

"Could Samir be involved in the other murders?" Alek said softly in Russian, knowing that Ezee wouldn't understand him.

I shook my head, ignoring Ezee's questioning look. "Think we can dig out some of those bullet fragments? Maybe I can get a trace on the assassin."

"He another sorcerer?" Ezee asked as Alek pulled out a folding knife and bent down over the still warm asphalt.

"Maybe," I said. "This was definitely magic. Like something out of an anime, right? Exploding paper. Whatever was written on it looked like Japanese."

"Should we be standing in the open like this then?" Ezee glanced around again, fidgeting with the strap on his messenger bag.

"Go to your office," I said. "I think Alek the giant tiger freaked the assassin out for now. Hopefully no one saw that," I added.

Alek lifted a shoulder in a half-shrug. "I sensed no one else around. Just the person driving that car. He seemed alone."

"Eh, it's Wylde," Ezee added with a tentative smile. "Besides, almost nobody is on campus and the dorms are on the other side of the hill. I doubt anyone will even report a gunshot."

He took off up the hill after I assured him that yes, we would be fine. Alek carefully handed me pieces of the bullet, the metal warm in my palm.

"It was a .308," he said, as though that would mean anything to me.

I tugged on my magic, wincing at the headache starting to form. I pictured the metal, the hand that must have last touched it, the environment it would have been in, maybe touching all its little bullet buddies. I fed my magic into that, pressing my will into the spell, telling it to trace its friends, trace its owner.

And I got zip, nilch, nada back. It was as though the bullet had come into being seconds before it got melted in the explosion. Fire is a good cleansing agent, but I should have been able to pick up something, even if it were uselessly vague.

"It's clean," I said, dropping the fragments in disgust. "Like, magically it has no signature at all. Like it never touched anyone." A chill went through me. This assassin knew what he or she was doing. I would have been willing to stake my game store on the guess that this assassin had hunted and killed magic users and supernaturals before.

The exploding note and the fact that they'd been willing to shoot at me in broad daylight, with friends around, was more disturbing. It meant that collateral damage wasn't really a concern for the killer.

Once again, just being me was putting everyone around me in danger. F-M-fucking-L.

"Jade," Alek said softly, stepping up to me. He wrapped his arms around me and I didn't resist. "We will find and destroy this assassin and send Samir his head."

"I love it when you go all Conan on me," I said, resisting the urge to rub my nose on his chest. "Then we will listen to the lamentations of his women, right?"

I pushed away from him and sighed. "At least now I know someone is trying to kill me. I'll be more ready for it next time. I hope." All I wanted was a ten-year nap, but I had a store to run. I couldn't leave Harper there forever. She'd just come kick my ass again. "Take me home," I said.

I took a quick shower and changed. Alek hadn't wanted to leave me, but I pointed out he had work to do that was more important than babysitting someone who could take care of herself. I promised to be careful with windows and walking out doors, as ridiculous as that sounded. I knew he had a point.

I made it down to the shop just in time to stop a fistfight. Harper looked about ready to kill one of my regulars. Trevor came by and hung out on Friday and Saturday afternoons, painting minis that we sold on eBay in trade for me keeping him supplied with comics.

"You cannot be serious," she was shrieking at him. She had a stack of comics in her hands, where she'd been setting out the new releases on the wide display rack I kept for them, but she was now brandishing them like they were going to be weapon number one if fisticuffs happened.

"If your brain hadn't been fried by all the cartoons you watch, you'd understand," Trevor said. He was grinning slyly, clearly baiting Harper. Man had a deathwish.

"Get out of my goddamn store…" Harper started to say, her pale skin turning an awesome blotchy shade of scarlet.

"Woah," I said. "It's my store, furball, and no one has to go. What is going on?"

"He said," Harper started, then paused to take a dramatic breath. "He said that the Punisher would kick Batman's ass in a fight."

"You said that?" I turned to Trevor.

"I was just pointing out the advantages that the Punisher has." Sensing danger, he backed up and slid behind the card table he set up to paint on, putting it between him and us.

I turned and walked to the tall bookshelf that held the graphic novels. I pulled out the hardbound slipcase of the *Absolute Dark Knight*. Slamming it down on the table in front of him, I leaned in close enough to tell he'd been eating Cheetos for lunch.

"You like painting minis here? You like the free comics?" I said, trying to keep the smile off my face.

"Sure do, boss," he said, his expression scared but his brown eyes dancing with humor.

"Then put your hand here and repeat after me," I said, indicating the slipcase. "I solemnly swear that Bruce Wayne is the bestest superhero ever and I will never profane his name or legacy by suggesting anyone could kick his ass. Because they can't. Because he is the fucking BATMAN."

He managed to repeat what I'd said with only a minimum of giggles. For a man who worked nights at a truck stop and still lived in his parents' basement, Trevor had a lot of pride. I then looked at Harper. "Good enough?"

"Fine," she said, rolling her eyes. She turned back to putting away the comics and I returned the hardcover to its spot.

"So, saw Alek dropped you off," Harper said, coming over to the counter as I booted up my laptop, hoping to lose myself in translation work.

"We talked," I said.

"And? You guys okay now?"

"Yeah. Maybe. We'll see." I shrugged. A chunk of hair fell into my face. I had tried to braid it all back like usual, but the part that had been obliterated by the bullet was too short to stay tucked in. I'd need to French braid it or something. Another annoyance.

"What happened to your hair?" Harper reached over and tugged on the short chunk.

I glanced past her at the back of the store where Trevor had pulled his painting table and was setting up to get to work. He was human, so I doubted he could hear us. I still lowered my voice down to a near whisper, knowing Harper's preternatural senses would pick it up just fine.

"Someone took a shot at me today, at the college," I whispered. I didn't really want to worry her, but Ezee had been there, so it wasn't like I'd be able to keep it a secret from Levi or Harper. I was somewhat surprised he hadn't texted both of them ASAP afterward.

Then I saw the total lack of surprise in Harper's face. Ezee had texted her. Bastard.

"Yeah, I wondered if you'd tell me yourself," she whispered back. "You are still coming to dinner tonight though. No getting out of that."

"It isn't a good idea," I said. "Who knows when that assassin will try again? I would just put your mom and Max in danger. Plus I think Levi is bringing Junebug. That's too many people I care about in one place for me to risk it."

"Bullshit. Who better to protect you?" She made a face at me. "You can't live your life looking over your shoulder, remember? We're here to watch your back. If you don't show up, I'll tell Mom why and she'll bring the whole damn thing to you, and you know it. Besides, you warded the shit out of the Henhouse. There's probably no safer place in town."

She had a point there. I had been practicing wards by layering them all around Harper's mother's bed and breakfast. It was remote enough I could work magic without fear of random discovery, and often had all my friends gathered there. And, until he'd taken off, Alek had been living there in his house trailer, which had been another reason to make sure the place was protected.

"Fine," I muttered. "Now will you please let me work?"

She looked like she had more questions, but just sighed and grabbed her own laptop off the counter, retreating to the oversized chair she liked to game in.

I closed my eyes and tried to picture the word written on the paper, but it hung outside my memory, eclipsed by the explosion, the press of power on my body. Japanese, though, I was almost sure of that. Painted with ink; I remembered the shape of the symbol, the brush lines, the flow of it. I gave up eventually and opened my email.

The day wore on without anyone trying to kill me or accuse me of murder, or any other shenanigans. I was almost lulled into thinking things might stay normal. Almost. I pulled the shades on the front windows, though with the displays and the posters up, it was very difficult to see directly into the story anyway. I had a hard time turning my back on the windows or doors, and for the first time in forever, I actually locked the rear door. It isn't paranoia when someone is actually trying to kill you.

Alek showed up just before I was ready to close for the night at seven. During slow seasons like this I usually didn't bother keeping the place open later than that. Wylde during the non-school year is usually a sleepy little town where everyone stays in after dark. Maybe because many of its residents are things that go bump in the night. Or run around howling at the moon.

It was getting dark as I hustled Harper out with a promise I'd be at dinner in an hour. Alek slipped in the door as I was preparing to lock up.

"Find anything?" I asked.

He shook his head. "I am keeping my inquiries soft at the moment. I do not want to draw attention to the missing humans if I can. Liam, Ulfr's oldest son and the interim alpha, knows the whole story. I questioned him closely and am convinced he is uninvolved and deeply invested in the Peace staying intact. Henry, Dorrie's mate, also knows some of it. He also appears uninvolved."

"So what's our next step?" I said, emphasizing the "our" part of it.

"I am going to try to trace the Lansings' steps. I will start at their house and then follow the route Vivian said they would likely take to Bear Lake. Perhaps I can find where they were taken, and track the killer or killers from there." Alek rubbed at his neck, rolling his shoulders. It was the only indication he gave of how tired he must be. I doubted he had gotten much more sleep than I had last night.

"Great, let me lock up and I'll come with you." I latched onto the excuse not to put my friends in danger, and the excuse to be doing something, anything, that wasn't just waiting for someone to try to kill me again.

"No," Alek said. "I can do this on my own. I might be gone for hours. If something happens here, you may be needed. Liam has your number, and Harper's, since you have such terrible phone luck." He smiled at that last part, pulling my cell phone from his coat pocket. He must have retrieved it at the pool. I hadn't even remembered it after the whole "being shot at" thing happened.

"Thanks," I said. "You sure you don't want company?"

"It is likely another dead end," he said, folding his hand around mine.

"The Council's visions aren't giving you some help on this? What did they show you?" I asked.

The troubled look returned to his eyes, and he bent and kissed my knuckles. "Nothing useful," he murmured. "I'll see you tomorrow."

"Call me if you find anything," I said, uneasy with his answer, his almost defeated posture.

"I promise," he said as he turned away and left.

I watched him go, then locked my door and flipped the sign to closed.

"We got a last-minute guest, but he's out taking pictures," Max said as he walked me into the big house that served as home and business for Rosie, Max and Harper's mother.

Rosie wasn't Max's real mother. She'd taken the boy in when he was just a pup. Harper didn't know where Rosie had come by him; Max was just one of the strays that Rosie had adopted. She had a big heart, Harper's mom did.

I had a sneaking suspicion that I was another stray she'd taken in, but I was too flattered by inclusion in this odd little shifter family to ask outright.

"Oh yeah?" I said to Max when I realized I was being too quiet. "Photographer. That's cool."

He continued talking at me, telling me about dinner and how he was going to take the photographer out on a ride tomorrow. Only thing Max loved more than his big sister was horses. Weird for a wolf, in my mind, but the horses seemed to love him right back and not mind at all that he was, at heart, a predator. They were strays too, rescued from auction blocks all over Idaho. Who knows? Maybe even the horses knew a good thing when they saw it.

The Henhouse Bed and Breakfast was a good thing. The house had that old country feel, lots of wood, handmade quilts on the beds, a big country kitchen with whitewashed cupboards, a giant gas stove, and an original riverstone fireplace with cooking hearth. The land and original ranch had been grandfathered into the River of No Return Wilderness area. The house and barn were relics of another time, slowly built on and updated by Rosie. I didn't know how old she really was, but I was guessing she'd settled this land a long, long time ago.

Dinner smelled delicious, some kind of thick, spicy game stew bubbling in a huge pot, and the yeasty, comforting scent of fresh-baked bread. I helped Harper set the huge dining table while Junebug, Levi's owl-shifter wife, and Ezee bustled around the kitchen with Rosie directing with the efficiency of a drill sergeant.

I knew from the looks I was getting that Ezee had told Levi and Rosie at the very least about the assassination attempt. We should have been eating outside on the huge porch, enjoying the last dying warmth of summer. No one said a word about us eating inside and I swallowed my own protests. If being in here kept me safer, it would keep them safer, too.

As we bantered, bustled, and tried to stay out of each other's way, I felt at home, almost forgetting that a giant target was painted on my back.

Ezee snagged a roll from the basket as Junebug brought it out to the table. The tiny woman admonished him, her amber eyes flashing with laughter as he pretended to put the roll back and instead tossed it to Max at the last moment.

"We're about to eat, and I think I hear our guest coming in," Junebug said. She grinned and ruined her stern look, shoving her long blond hair away from her face as she tried to leap up and snag the roll. Levi caught her waist and lifted her in a smooth motion and she snagged the roll from midair. She smiled up at him as she returned it to the basket and, bending, he kissed the tip of her nose.

Nez Perce punk mechanic and tiny blond hippy. Levi was all sarcastic humor and moody edges, Junebug smiles and earthy mothering that rivaled Rosie's. If the world had room for their love in it, maybe there was hope for me, too. I pushed away the weird longing that rose up inside. I was getting maudlin in my old age, apparently. Introspection had never been my strong suit.

I heard the front door open and turned, pulling on my magic for a moment as the back of my neck prickled.

A slender Japanese man entered, pausing in the doorway. He had a camera bag slung around his neck. The guest. I let go of my magic, sensing nothing off about him. He hadn't triggered any of my wards, so he was human as well. Just a guy.

I smiled at him and Rosie emerged from the kitchen.

"Please, Mr. Kami, come in," she said, bowing politely as she wiped her hands on her apron.

"I do not wish to intrude," he said in accented but very fluent English. "This is your family time."

"You aren't intruding. Please join us for dinner." Rosie smiled at him and the small man smiled back, unable to resist her charm.

We made introductions all around, and everyone settled in. For a few minutes peace reigned as food was passed around and dished out. I looked around the table and felt something, like a small chip of myself, settle in my heart. Family.

The warm feeling was only slightly dampened by remembering what always seemed to happen to my families.

I found myself studying Mr. Kami, who was seated across the table and one down from where I was. His face was lined enough to place him in his forties at least, with his hair pulled into a topknot that reminded me of old samurai movies. He wore loose black pants and a long-sleeved dark green shirt. He'd hung his camera bag off the chair behind him.

There was nothing unusual about him. His face was bland, almost forgettable. His eyes were dark, though not as dark as mine. He was tanned, more so than heritage would dictate, which fit with a man who spent lots of time outdoors taking pictures. His fingernails were trimmed and he ate with a polite tidiness that drew no attention.

Maybe it was because someone had tried to kill me. Maybe it was the Lansings' deaths or Dorrie's poisoning. I felt on edge, paranoia damaging what should have been a happy evening. I shoved the feeling down and decided to make small talk.

"Kami is an unusual surname," I said. "Where in Japan did you grow up?"

His eyes flicked to me and he brought his napkin up, carefully wiping his mouth and finishing chewing before he spoke.

"A tiny village in the Oki Shoto islands," he said. "It is very remote."

"I'd love to go to Japan," Harper said. "I've been to South Korea for tournaments, but never any further."

"Tournaments?" Mr. Kami asked.

"Oh God, don't get her started," Levi said with a mock groan.

"But I am curious. Please tell," Mr. Kami said.

Which led into an explanation about what Harper did for a living with videogames that Mr. Kami listened to with very polite attention.

I'd heard of the Oki Shoto islands. Kami means paper, or spirit. It's a weird last name. Japan has a huge diversity of surnames, it's true, but it was the only odd thing about a man who was otherwise completely normal-seeming. Human. Boring. Everything about him from his appearance to his mannerisms said "nothing to see here, move along."

I was so fucked up that his sheer normalness bugged me. Or maybe it was that curling slip of paper earlier. What were the odds that in a tiny town like Wylde, someone would show up using Japanese on a spell scroll and it not be remotely related to the one Japanese foreigner in town? I didn't believe in coincidence. Not today.

I closed my eyes for a moment, listening with my other senses to the conversation, to the people around me. I pulled on my magic, spooling up a thread of power from the huge well within. I touched my wards, letting my consciousness spiral to the outermost circles around the property. Nothing unusual. I pulled myself back in, listening with magically enhanced senses to my friends. I felt their own thrumming power, the soft rhythms of their hearts, the tickling feel of their sleeping animal selves. I could identify each just by his or her energy signature, that metaphysical something that helped define what they were. This awareness of life power in others, this second sense was a gift, of sorts, from an asshole murdering warlock whose heart I'd eaten to save Rosie and Ezee's lives only a few months before.

Mr. Kami, however, didn't even register. It was like he wasn't there. He might have been part of the chair on which he sat for all my metaphysical senses could tell.

He should have shown up. I could sense the horses in their stalls, sense the fat tabby cat out on the porch swing. Not Mr. Kami. He had less presence inside my wards, against my magic, than a cat. I opened my eyes and looked at him.

Then, deliberately, carefully, I prodded him with a touch of my power. To a human's senses, it should have felt like something brushed against him, a phantom touch. A truly oblivious human, like our friend and fellow gamer Steve, might have felt nothing at all.

Mr. Kami tensed and flicked his dark eyes to me. For a moment it was like a mask slipped out of place and his gaze went beetle-black and hard, intense and focused like a predator's. Then the bland look came back, but I felt an answering push of power. Just a touch, the smell and feel of it hot and alien.

Ink and earth, smoke and gunpowder.

I was sitting at dinner with the man who had tried to blow off my head only hours earlier.

I smiled at him, all teeth. "Have you seen the barn?" I asked him. I wanted to take his head off right here, but he had magic. I couldn't predict what he would do. His actions earlier had indicated a total disregard for collateral damage and we were sitting around a table full of people I cared about.

Not exactly an advantage.

"Yes," he said, his mask back in place. "Max showed me earlier. It is very nice. This is a very nice place."

I gathered my power, letting it spread through me, ready to blast him or shield my friends. "We should go outside," I said to him in Japanese.

"I am fine where I am," he responded in the same as he leaned back, scooting his chair out a small ways. He draped one hand casually over the back of Junebug's chair next to him. "How did you recognize me?"

"You were too invisible," I said. I wanted to zort him right out of his chair, blast him away and end the threat, but I didn't know what magic he had, what it might do. There were too many people.

"Jade," Levi said.

I didn't dare look at him and risk the man in front of him making a move. "This man is the killer," I said instead, switching to Nez Perce.

I had engaged in long discussions on the dying out of the Sahaptian language with Ezee, so I knew he at least would understand. And Junebug had been an academic, studying Northwestern Native cultures before she fell in love with a wolverine-shifter mechanic and took up pottery.

Levi, Ezee, and Junebug all tensed. Beside me, Max stood up.

"Anyone want more ice in their water?" he said, too brightly.

Mr. Kami's right hand slipped beneath the table. I took the risk and threw pure force straight at him, driving into him with my will, wanting to crush him like a bug. As he flew backward and flipped out of his chair, magic flared to life, burning sigils appearing in the air around him and turning aside the brunt of my blast.

On the periphery of my vision I saw my friends all leave their chairs, moving with the graceful speed only shifters can achieve. Ezee and Levi shifted, a huge coyote and wolverine materializing. They sprang at the assassin, snarling.

"No," I called out as I struggled to my feet, shoving my chair away.

Glittering kunai filled the air as the assassin leapt onto the table. I threw shields up around my friends. Fire started to swirl around the killer's body, sigils spinning faster and faster. Heat blasted over me and I pushed more power into my shields. The table began to burn.

I had to get him out of the house or he would just burn it down around us. I slammed more force into him as my friends attacked. The assassin jumped away, moving out of the dining room and into the front entry.

I grabbed the pitcher of water off the table as I followed and threw it in his direction, turning the water into a thin spear of ice. Magic raged through me, my blood singing with it, but I felt the edge of fatigue as well. Keeping his fire contained, my friends shielded, and throwing magic at him was taking a quick toll on me.

I gritted my teeth as the front door flew open and he dashed through it, the ice spear melting away before it hit him. He threw more kunai at me, the small dark blades glancing off my shields.

Bits of paper tied to the loop at the ends fluttered as the knives bounced and fell. I threw magic tendrils at them, mage-handing them back out the door as quickly as I could. Explosions rocked the house and I stumbled, smoke and heat filling my nose. A furry body raced past me.

I made it through the smoking ruins of the front entry, rage rising inside me. The assassin was running for his car. He spun as I sprang down the steps, and he fired a pistol at me. The shots hit my shields like punches from giant fists, the force shoving me backward, off my feet.

A fox, her body a streak of red in my smoke-blurred vision, leapt straight through his wreath of flames and latched onto his arm.

Harper.

I rolled to my feet and ran at the assassin. He threw Harper aside as though she were a puppy, not a hundred-pound fox. His lips moved and he thrust his arms out. His shirt curled and burned, the pieces lifting and turning into their own slips of dark paper, sigils flaming to life on the ruins of his clothing. I poured everything I had into my shields as a wave of flame rushed at me.

Belatedly, I remembered the house behind me, the people who might be there. Harper somewhere to the side of me, a crumpled form in the dry summer grass.

My shields took the heat and I threw my will into directing it upward, toward the sky, toward nothing that it could burn and hurt and kill. My eyes squeezed shut against the heat. I held my breath, ignoring the stench of burning hair as I spread my shields as thin as I could, trying to funnel the flame wave away from everything. Away from the people I kept failing to protect.

Pain radiated through my forearms and I felt my own clothing catching fire. It wasn't going to be enough. I needed more power, another answer. No time. I hung on, gripping my twenty-sided talisman with hands gone numb from pain, pouring all my strength into blocking the flames as the unfamiliar magic roared over me, resisting, almost alive, hungry for death.

And then, as it had before with the explosion in the parking lot, it suddenly ceased. Blood roared in my ears instead of fire.

I raised my head, catching sight of the retreating taillights of the assassin's car. Again. He turned a corner, speeding off. I had no energy to go after him. I wanted to breathe. To curl up in a bath of ice and forget what fire tasted like. My body vibrated with spent power. With terror. With pain. My arms were raw, skin bubbling into blisters even as I stared at it, trying to gather my mind back into itself.

Rosie ran past me, toward a charred shape in the smoldering grass to the side of the driveway. Then she started screaming.

Harper was alive, barely. Her scorched chest rose and fell in uneven breaths. Clumps of charred hair fell off her as Levi and I carefully got her moved onto a blanket and brought into the house.

"Why isn't she shifting?" I asked, ignoring the pain in my hands and arms as the blanket rubbed on raw, burnt patches of skin.

"She's not conscious," Levi said. "She's breathing though. Her body will start to heal."

"Can you do anything?" Max asked me. "Heal her?"

I shook my head. Healing was complicated. I didn't know anatomy or what her healthy skin was supposed to be like exactly. I was scared to try using my magic that way. I'd attempted to heal Wolf once and had failed miserably, my magic sliding uselessly off her bloody chest.

Wolf appeared as though thinking of her had called her. I wanted to curse at her, ask her where she had been, but she couldn't have stopped this. The assassin was human—using some kind of magic, sure, but not a magical being himself, not enough that she would have been able to help.

Still, part of me thought she could have at least warned me. She should have smelled the magic on him. Instead she'd been absent. I felt betrayed, but shoved it away. Irrational anger wouldn't save Harper.

"Max," Rosie said. "Go help Ezekiel put out the fires."

He glared at her but left, throwing a last worried look over his shoulder at Harper.

We put her on a bed in the first-floor guest room. Her fox body was small for a shifter, her normally red and glossy fur charred away in ugly weals, burned to brown and black and patches of raw red flesh.

Guilt swamped me as I stood there, helpless.

"I shouldn't have come tonight," I said.

"You don't know what he would have done if you hadn't," Rosie said. "Don't start blaming yourself, dearie. If we start that game then Harper shouldn't have run out the door like an idiot. That man was bad news. He is the one to blame. He set my baby on fire."

"But only because I was here," I said, turning to her. My vision blurred as tears leaked out my eyes, tears of rage, tears of guilt. "And I didn't stop him. How can you look at her and not hate me?"

"You saved me from the slowest, most terrible death I could ever envision. You risked your life, your freedom to protect my family. As far as I am concerned, that makes you family." Rosie's mouth set into a line and her hazel eyes were uncomfortably kind, full of a deep understanding that wrapped around me like a physical presence.

"Family," she continued. "Family don't give up on family just because things get dangerous. Azalea risked her life for you, same as you'd risk your life for her. Don't belittle that choice by pretending you could make it for her. You don't have that right."

She squared her shoulders as I shut my mouth on any protest I would make. I stared down at my burnt arms, my flaking and crisped shirt. Something was hard and uncomfortably hot in my pocket. A fried plastic smell leached from my jeans.

I pulled out my cell phone, wincing. It was dead, totally slagged by heat.

"Jade," Rosie said.

I looked up. Levi had slipped out of the room. It was only Rosie and I now, with Harper's heavily breathing body on the bed between us. At least she was still breathing.

"Go get a clean shirt, clean those burns off. She isn't going to die."

"I'm already healing," I muttered, the guilt not quite gone. I did as she asked, however, slipping up the stairs to Harper's room. Peeling off the remains of my clothes sucked more than I want to say, but the burns on my arms were turning pink now, the blisters fading down into the skin almost as quickly as they'd appeared.

As my head cleared, rage replaced the guilt. I didn't know where Mr. Kami had gone, but I was going to find him. I was going to end him.

I washed my face off, biting down a scream as the water hit freshly healing skin. My hair wasn't as damaged as I'd feared, but it would take a true shower and a lot of conditioner to return it to some semblance of pretty. I left it as it was and went back downstairs.

Harper wasn't a fox anymore. Her human skin was clean of burns, but she lay on the bed whimpering under her breath as Rosie covered her with a clean quilt. Her green eyes were open and clear. Relief dumped the rest of the adrenaline from my veins and weighed me down.

"Hey, furball," I said, sitting on the edge of the bed. "You okay?"

"I will be," she said. She winced, as though it hurt to talk, and her voice was rough.

"I thought you told me that shifting healed you?" I said with narrowed eyes.

Her lips formed a faint smile. "It does, eventually. I still feel pain through the link though, am still weak. I didn't want you worrying about us anymore than you already do though. So I kinda fudged the truth a bit, sorry."

"I'm sorry I didn't protect you," I said.

"I ain't dead yet," Harper said. "'Sides, I totally got a chunk of that guy. Won't be throwing ninja stars with that arm anytime soon."

She was right about that, unless he knew spells that healed, which I supposed wasn't unlikely. I'd seen similar things, though not in real life outside of shops where they weren't truly imbued with magic. Ofuda, like you'd find at a Shinto shrine. Or Omamori, protective Japanese talismans. Nothing I'd seen outside of animated movies looked like what the assassin had managed. Spells inscribed on paper. Fire and ink. I suspected the sheets of paper stuck to his body were for physical enhancements. It sucked he was trying to kill me, because his kind of magical practice was fascinating. Maybe I'd ask him questions before I kicked his ass.

Chuckling at that, I imagined myself like a monologueing villain, giving the enemy the chance to recover and surprise me. Maybe I wouldn't be holding another conversation with Mr. Kami. I wondered for a moment why I cast myself as the villain in my head, but shoved the rising tide of dark thoughts away for later examination.

"You promise you'll be okay? And never do that again?" I asked.

"Yeah, yeah," she said, her eyes slipping shut. "I learned my lesson. Fire bad. Tree pretty." She closed her eyes and her breathing slowed, deepened.

If she was cognizant enough to make a *Buffy the Vampire Slayer* reference, I figured she just might live after all. I watched Harper sleep for a few minutes until I heard voices. Reluctantly, I rose and left the room. Levi, Ezee, Max, and Junebug all trooped back into the dining room, spent fire extinguishers in hand.

"Fire is out; don't think we're at risk of a wildfire," Levi said.

I nodded, looking around the charred dining room. The table was a mess of burn scars and smashed dishes. The chairs were overturned. Next to one was a familiar bag. Mr. Kami's camera bag.

I picked it up, reaching for my magic. The bag seemed normal at first, then that normalcy fell away and the alien touch of foreign magic brushed against my power as I tried to link this object to its own.

It wasn't the smoke and ink power of the assassin that touched me, but another power, one I had once been very familiar with.

Cool sweetness flowed through the bag, a seductive song against my senses, like watching the ocean waves roll in and out. Deep, vast, a power that knew no limits and would take you into its embrace with hardly a ripple.

Samir.

I dropped the bag, my heart punching against my ribs. Without thinking I ripped into the magic there, the physical bag itself as well, smashing in, rending it piece by piece and turning the pieces to ash.

"Jade, Jade!" Ezee's voice finally penetrated my fear, my hatred.

I looked up at him, amazed to find myself on my knees, a smoking pile of ashes at my feet.

"It was evil," I said, aware I looked totally crazed.

"It's dead now," he said.

It was. And with it any chance I had of linking it to the assassin. I took tiny consolation in the fact that it was unlikely I could have anyway, not with Samir's power all over it.

"What was it?" Max asked, poking at the ashes with his sneaker.

"A container," I guessed. "For my heart."

"Gross," he said.

A search of the room that Rosie had rented to the assassin revealed nothing, not a stitch of clothing or a metaphysical trace. I had already half expected that.

Weary to the bone, I made my way back to the room where Harper still slept, and collapsed into a chair. Her steady breathing reassured me, but I still wanted to stay, to keep watch. I didn't trust that the assassin wouldn't come back.

Rosie sat on the other side of Harper for a while, knitting. I heard the others moving around out in the front rooms, cleaning up. I almost went to help them, but my body had decided that sitting was all I was going to be good for at the moment. Exhaustion crawled over me, and I found myself drifting off. At some point, Rosie put a blanket over me, and Harper's soft breathing carried me into uneasy sleep.

Alek woke me with a kiss. The sun streamed through the window and I had a hell of a crick in my neck. The clock on the nightstand said it was after ten in the morning. I opened my eyes, half convinced I was dreaming.

He looked far too tired for this to be a dream, however. His ice-blue eyes were bloodshot and shadows had taken up residence below them. I looked from him over to where Harper still slept.

"Max told me what happened," Alek said.

"Rosie promises she'll be okay," I said.

"She will. Come have breakfast."

I sat in the kitchen and picked at my pancakes for a few minutes under Alek and Rosie's watchful gazes, then pushed the plate away. I was too keyed up to eat much. I wanted to lay some hurt on someone, preferably a damned ninja assassin someone, but I'd settle for whoever killed the Lansings.

"You get anywhere?" I asked Alek, though I was guessing he hadn't from his exhausted and frustrated expression.

"No," he said, then switched to Russian as he glanced at Rosie. "I could find no trace of them. Their car is missing. But no unusual scents at their house, no sign of struggle. Nothing on the road between here and Bear Lake, or at their cabin."

Rosie slipped out of the room with a murmur about looking in on Harper. I felt bad about talking in a language she didn't speak in front of her, but Alek clearly wanted to keep the murders as quiet as possible.

"Bear Lake? You drive all night?" I asked. It was obvious he had. I sighed.

"Most of it," he said. "I have Liam and a few of his pack he trusts, and who I vetted, out looking for the car. If they were taken anywhere near Wylde, the wolves should be able to pick up a trail." He didn't look as hopeful as his words sounded. He just looked tired.

"You need sleep," I said. "Where is your trailer?"

"On the side, in the RV parking." He drained the last of his cup of tea and started to rise.

"Rosie won't begrudge you a room, you know."

Alek shook his head. "Too much to do."

"Too many ways to fuck up if you don't sleep," I said. "What about that other Justice? Shouldn't she be helping?"

His expression soured, and he sighed. "Vivian told her about the murders, said Eva came and asked about Dorrie. She came to the Lansings' house before I did—I smelled her presence there. She does not wish to work directly with me, I do not think. We do not get along."

"What about the Council? They not giving you useful guidance? You'd think they'd want you two to work together since this Peace is so important."

"Yes," he said, his jaw clenching. "Perhaps." He shook his head at my questioning look.

"Will a shower with me cheer you up?" I asked. It was a shameless move, but he needed rest, needed to relax. We both did.

We borrowed one of the empty guest rooms on the second floor. The shower cheered up both of us and we lost ourselves in skin and comfort and heat for a little while. He pulled on his underwear, then crawled into the bed when I pointed. I tugged on my borrowed teeshirt and jeans, then pulled a quilt over him, and lay down on top of it.

Alek's arms came around me and he tucked my head under his chin.

"I fucked up," I said softly. "I almost got everyone killed again."

"Don't blame the victim," he said. "That assassin doesn't care about collateral damage. He was here, in this place, for a reason. Perhaps Samir wishes for your friends to be killed, to be hurt, as well. This is very like him, yes?"

"Are you trying to be comforting?" I muttered. I shook my head, rubbing it against his chin, and took a deep breath, inhaling Alek's vanilla and musk scent.

"I meant it in a more general way," I added, trying to order my thoughts. "I have been so defensive. Yesterday, when he shot at me, I ducked. Then I threw up a shield. I didn't blast his car off the road. I didn't try to go after him. I just went for cover, went for minimizing damage. And last night, I did the same. I hesitated when I should have just struck for a kill. And then I used so much power shielding and none attacking."

Somehow I knew that Alek might understand what I was thinking, what I was trying to say, that he, more than anyone in my life, would get my desire to stop reacting. To start acting.

"You think if you had acted more quickly, gone on the offensive, Harper would not be hurt?" he said softly.

"Yes."

"You might be right."

Okay, that stung a little. I mean, it was what I was thinking, but hearing someone else say it hurt.

"Ouch," I said, pulling away and sitting up.

He tucked his arms behind his head and looked up at me.

"You are afraid of your power," he said. It wasn't phrased as a question.

"A little, yes," I admitted. "There is so much of it, and it's growing all the time. When I was younger I just stuck to little stuff until Samir came along, trying out spells I found in the DnD manual, but I didn't do too much. I was afraid even then, afraid I would hurt people. I don't feel like I have control, I don't know what my limits are until I hit them, I don't even know if those are real limits or if my brain is just imposing them to save some shred of my psyche. I'm terrified of hurting people around me." The words flowed out of me in a rush, leaving behind a strange relief that I had finally said them aloud.

"With great power comes great responsibility," he said, nodding sagely.

"Did you just quote *Spider-Man* at me?" I raised an eyebrow, impressed.

"*Spider-Man*? No. Voltaire. Or, technically, Jesus, if you believe the gospel of Luke. I believe he said, 'To whom much is given, much is expected.'"

Oh. Right. That made more sense. Alek was still cute when he was smug and all full of the brains.

"Well, Uncle Ben said it, too," I said, making a face at him.

He smiled but it didn't last, his serious expression returning.

"You did what you felt was right, for you, for that moment," he said. "There is no shame in that. Learn from it, from these doubts and feelings and fears. Next time, make a different decision. Just remember to always decide. Inaction is death."

"I don't know if I can be a killer," I blurted, saying the words that had hovered in my mind since I watched, helpless, as my father died in front of me, torn apart because of my decisions. If I had killed Not Afraid. If I had killed Sky Heart. If I had never gone back. If if if. I was terrified that all the solutions I saw looked like death for someone.

I was terrified that part of me wanted that death. Killing Bernie hadn't sucked. I didn't like his slimy, psychotic memories living in my head, but I didn't regret eating his heart and ending him for even a second.

And that scared me, too.

"Liar," Alek murmured, his voice incredibly soft, almost a purr. Looking into his eyes felt like falling into the sky.

I sank back down, laying my head on his chest. His arms came back around me.

"I don't know," I said. "I'm tired of death, but I'm tired of worrying so much about it, about causing it when it seems like my enemies stack up and don't give a shit. I'm tired of every problem looking like a nail. Does it get easier?"

"Does what get easier?" he asked.

"Killing," I said.

"Yes," he said, his voice deep and sad. "It does."

After a while, we both slept.

8

"Lean on Me" by Bill Withers was playing as I sleepily lifted my head.

"Fuck is that?" I mumbled, lost for a moment as to where I was. I knew the warm body trying to move out from under me was Alek. Then the rest of it flowed into my half-conscious brain.

"My phone," Alek said. He lifted me off him and grabbed his pants from the floor, fishing his phone out of them. "Yes?"

I smiled at his choice of ringtone. I'd missed his sense of humor. The room was dim, and I looked out the window toward the barn. Long shadows from the trees clung like tentacles along its red roof. The sun was setting.

"We're coming now," Alek said, all sleepiness gone from his voice and his posture.

"What is it?" I asked as he shoved his phone into his pants pocket and started dressing with preternatural speed. He didn't bother with his sweater, pulling on his undershirt as he checked for his car keys.

"Liam has been murdered," he said.

We raced down the stairs, pausing to throw on our shoes in the entry. I glanced toward the room where Harper was, realizing I was leaving her without my protection. I hesitated and Alek looked back at me, the front door already open.

Rosie appeared in the door to Harper's room. "Trouble?" she said.

"Yeah," I said, glancing at Alek. "But I can stay."

"Harper ate three sandwiches and went back to sleep an hour ago," Rosie said, making a shooing motion. "She'll be fine. We'll all be fine. Go watch the Justice's back."

"Jade?" Alek said.

"All right," I said. I turned and followed him out.

In the shadows of the porch, I spied Levi and Junebug sitting in Adirondack chairs. Junebug had a carving knife and a length of rosewood in her hands, whittling away. Levi had a hunting rifle across his knees. They both nodded to us as we went by, heading for Alek's truck.

I expected Alek to drive us back to town and through to the other side, to head toward the Den where the Wylde pack lived. Instead he headed out farther along the road after leaving the offshoot that led to the Henhouse, taking us right along the edge of the wilderness. We pulled into the large turnaround and day-use lot at the Three Firs trailhead. Sheriff Lee's official SUV was pulled up there, along with at least four other vehicles.

There was enough daylight left to see the crowd gathered in the grassy area beyond the lot. I recognized a few of them, faces I knew from around town, but there were at least half a dozen men and women who I couldn't place as belonging in Wylde. Alek and I climbed out of the truck and I felt the suspicious looks and tension like a physical weight pressing on me.

I walked toward the crowd beside Alek, refusing to look down or away from any of the eyes that met mine. I was not prey. I was here because a Justice wanted me here. I was here because I wanted, no, *needed* to help. Someone had to remember the human side of things, to remember the Lansings in their unmarked graves. To use Alek's metaphor, I was here to help balance the scales.

Eva, the other Justice, stood near a tarp on the ground spread over I didn't want to know what, talking to Sheriff Lee. The sheriff was an American-born Chinese, her family was original to the non-Native settlement of the area. They had come to work the gold mines in the Dakotas and kept moving westward as time wore on. I didn't know how old she was, but I'd chatted with her a time or two in Brie's bakery and got the impression that she hadn't been one of the original family members to come to Idaho, but was born here, sometime inside this century.

Of course, with shifters, you never know.

I liked her. She was solid, steady, and good at making drunk tourists and college students back down from a fight. She kept a town full of supernaturals and shifters nearly crime-free. Well, with a few exceptions in the last year. Mainly *my* exceptions. I felt a pang of guilt and shoved it away.

Eva I did not like. I'd formed a snap impression of her, true, but her expression as Alek and I walked through the crowd of wolves toward her was sour and mean. Her dark blue eyes were hard and judgy. Yeah, I didn't think she'd become my favorite person anytime soon.

"What is she doing here?" she said, ignoring me and looking at Alek.

"She's with me," he said. "What happened?" He motioned at the tarp.

I breathed through my mouth, ignoring the buzz of flies and reek of death. More death. I was pretty sure I didn't want to see what was under that tarp.

"Someone murdered my brother," a woman said, stepping forward. "Someone is trying to kill their competition." She was tall and lean, with freckles and wheat-colored hair. Her face seemed familiar, but I was pretty sure we'd never officially met.

"Freyda," Alek said, and I got the feeling he was using her name both to calm her and for my benefit. "Perhaps this is less related to becoming the new alpha of alphas and more about the Peace," he suggested softly.

Murmurs went through the small crowd. I assumed some of them were visiting alphas. They looked diverse enough. Two tanned brothers with green eyes and thick beards, wearing jeans. A white man with silver in his light brown hair, dressed incongruously with the forest setting in business casual attire. A woman in a blue sundress with skin so dark it made mine look pale in comparison. All of them radiated power and control, their bearing reminding me a little of Alek. Definitely alphas.

Only one stood out, and he lurked a handful of paces back from the others, a dark-haired man who looked as though he hadn't slept in days and spent much of those eyes crying. His hair was crinkled and stuck in places, as though sweaty hands had run through it over and over. I guessed that this was Henry, Dorrie's mate. It must have been he who called Alek.

Freyda stared him in the eye, then slowly let her gaze drop. "There is no trail. We found sign of a pack, of at least three or four wolves, but they must have left in a vehicle. The trail ends." She pointed at the parking area.

"Sheriff." Alek turned to Lee. "May I see the body?"

She nodded even as Eva shook her head. "This is pointless. We should be questioning the sorceress." She glared at me.

Every set of eyes turned to me and the tension ramped up to epic levels. I was desperately thinking *don't be prey,* but at that moment I felt a lot like the rabbit in the shadow of an eagle. A pack of eagles. Hungry, angry eagles.

Yeah. Uh. Shit. So, that was out a cat out of the bag that wasn't ever going back in. I wanted to take the proverbial bag and smother that righteous bitch with it.

Alek stepped in front of me, all six and a half feet of him towering over everyone else, tension radiating from him, careful, controlled, but no less dangerous. Maybe more dangerous. Even Eva seemed to deflate a little under his sweeping icy gaze.

"Jade is here to help," he said, his words a growl.

I didn't need him fighting my battles for me, but on the other hand, this was his realm. I was no shifter; I had no idea about pack politics. Hell, apparently some of what Harper had been telling me about shifters wasn't even the full truth. I'd make her fix that, later. If we weren't all dead.

"Her number is the last one dialed in his phone," Lee said, bravely cutting in. "It is a valid question why he called her, what he said."

"I didn't talk to him," I said, moving back beside Alek so I could actually see the people I was talking to. "When did he call me?"

More importantly, *why* did he call me? I didn't say that aloud though. I remembered Alek saying something about giving Liam my number, telling him to call me if anything came up or he found the Lansings' car.

"Early this morning," Lee said.

"My phone kind of fell in a fire last night—it's been dead since nine pm or so."

"His heart is missing," Eva cut in. "I hear sorcerers like hearts."

"His heart is missing?" Alek asked, looking at Lee, not Eva.

I cast a glance around, wondering if others noticed the snub. From the speculative look the black woman and Freyda were giving Justice Eva, I thought at least some had.

"Yes. And his intestines. And a large chunk of his throat." Lee glanced at Freyda as she spoke, her light brown eyes soft and sad.

"Would you like to see?" Eva offered, her smile all teeth.

I swallowed bile and shook my head. I'd had way enough of death and dismemberment this week. Instead I took another step forward, meeting her eyes.

"I can prove I had nothing to do with this," I said. "You are a Justice, so you can tell when someone lies, right?"

The smile slid off her face as she nodded, her eyes narrowing with displeasure. She saw where I was going with this.

I looked around at the gathered wolves, making sure everyone was paying attention. Then I looked back at Eva and said, "I did not kill Liam son of Wulf. I did not talk to Liam at any time in the week before he died. I had no prior knowledge of his death, nor anything to do with it. Satisfied?"

She looked like she wanted to choke me, but she took a deep breath and glanced at Alek.

"Yes," she said grudgingly. "The sorceress is telling the truth."

"We should not be looking at outsiders," the man in the suit said. "This is clearly pack trouble."

"We will question the pack," Alek said. "We will question every alpha. If this is wolf-caused, those responsible will be brought to justice. It is what we do."

"And if the alpha responsible is not here?" asked one of the green-eyed brothers.

"Softpaw," Freyda said, eyes widening. "He has not come yet."

"Softpaw?" I asked Alek quietly.

"The Bitterroot pack alpha." It was Henry who answered me.

"The wild wolves live apart, and Softpaw was the only wolf to deny the Peace, to never acknowledge Wulf as the alpha of alphas," Freyda added.

"What is the point of reaffirming the Peace if not all sign? If all won't keep the Peace, why should any of us? The Council will not be happy," business-suit guy said.

"Do you know the will of the Council?" Alek said, moving toward the man, seeming to grow taller and wider with each step. "The Peace was good enough to last well over a century, even without the Bitteroot alpha. Do you think this Peace so weak, this situation so unimportant, that the Council would not care? If they did not care, would there be not one, but two Justices here?"

He paused and looked around, again meeting the eyes of everyone present. Except for Eva's.

"Whoever has done this, whether their goal is to disrupt the Peace or sabotage the true and fair competition for Alpha, he or she or they will be found. They will face the Council of Nine's Justice. Do you trust the Council's will?"

His words were clearly a trap, and everyone there flinched as he finished, his question hanging in the twilight. Everyone was looking at Alek except Eva, I noticed. She stared straight at me, her face twisted with a hatred I didn't understand. Then she met my eyes and a mask fell into place, her features smoothing out, her expression stern but bland.

"I trust the will of the Council," Freyda said. The others slowly followed with their own murmurs of agreement.

"Go," Alek said. "Calm your seconds. Talk to the other alphas. The wake will happen tomorrow as planned. We will not let a killer ruin Wulf's legacy."

They dispersed, except for Lee, Henry, and Eva.

"The body?" Alek said to Lee as the cars drove away. "Before we lose all the light?"

I sighed and steeled my nerves. Apparently I wasn't done seeing mutilated corpses this week. Awesomesauce.

Eva hovered but didn't interfere as Lee donned gloves and pulled back the tarp.

Liam had looked like his sister in life, but with more pronounced cheekbones and something familiar about the shape of his eyes that made me think he had Native American blood in him. His eyes were closed, his face spattered with blood but otherwise untouched.

His throat was missing, only a mess of torn flesh left holding his head on. I saw vertebrae in it and had to look away for a moment. It was a good thing I rarely dreamed. I could add this body to the list of horrible things I could never un-see.

His heart and a lot of his internal organs had been ripped out through a huge hole in his stomach. I was grateful for the dying sunlight, which softened the colors, painting everything in a muted palette and making it look waxy, a touch unreal.

"Tooth marks," Alek said. "Did he get a piece of his killer?"

"We think so," Lee said. She pulled an evidence bag out of her coat pocket. Inside was a tuft of black fur. "It is wolf, but not a scent any here recognized."

"Can you use this to track?" Alek said, taking it from her and turning to me.

"You would use her tainted magic?" Eva said.

"What is your problem with me?" I asked. "I don't even know you, and you really don't know me. I don't even know how you knew what I am."

"I met a sorceress once," Eva said. "I have never forgotten the way she smelled."

Sorceress. Female. So not Samir. I wondered who it was, if there was a chance the woman was still alive. I wished I could ask and expect a real answer.

"Well, she wasn't me. So get the fuck over yourself and let me help," I said.

Sheriff Lee and Henry both took a couple of steps back, their shock radiating like heat off their tense bodies.

"Eva," Alek said softly. "We must find the killer. Let her work."

Her eyes literally flashed, sheening with golden-brown light for a moment. I had the impression she wanted to shift, to let her wolf take me down. Or take Alek down. I pulled on my magic, letting it fill my veins, sing in my blood, and pool in my hands. *Let the bitch come at me*, I thought. I was ready to lay down a beating on the next person or thing to piss me off. I was too fucking tired of death and posturing and people trying to hurt me and the people I loved.

She turned abruptly and walked to the parking lot, climbing into one of the last three vehicles left. She snapped her fingers at Henry, and he looked at Alek with an apology in his puffy, reddened eyes, and left with Eva.

When the crunch of their tires on the gravel had faded, Alek looked at me. "Track?" he said.

Sheriff Lee watched with interest as I shook the fur out of the bag and into my palm. I pictured the wolf it must belong to, pushing my magic into the spell. Silver thread spiraled out from the fur, then hung in the air, pointing one way, then another, like a compass in the Bermuda Triangle.

I pushed more power into the spell, wondering if the owner of this fur was out of range. I had no idea what my range even was. I had never tracked someone more than maybe twenty miles. The spell fizzled, the connection too weak to form a link. Which was weird, since I'd formed stronger links off things people had only been in contact with. This was a piece of someone or something. It should have created a nice strong link. Unless…

"It's not working," I said. "I think this fur is very old. So old it has lost any real connection to its original body."

"Hmm," Lee said. Her lips pressed together and she looked skeptical. I didn't blame her. To her eyes it probably looked like I'd stared really hard at a bit of fur in my hand.

"Dead end," Alek said.

I slid the fur back into the bag. "Maybe science and the crime lab can tell you more," I said, handing it back to Lee.

Her laugh sounded tinny and bitter. "What do you think we are? CSI Idaho? Besides, this crime will never see a report."

Alek took his keys from his pocket and handed them to me. "Go back to your friends. I will help Lee, go talk to the other alphas, and then meet you later."

They were going to cover up another murder. I sighed. Somehow the sheriff being involved made it slightly less awful. Slightly. I knew that they couldn't bring this body to the country medical examiner, just as I had known before Alek made his case the other night that in the end, the Lansings' bodies couldn't be found by normals either. There was a whole world of magic and danger that humans couldn't see. I had a hard enough time wrapping my mind around this stuff. Universe knows what the rest of the world would do if faced with so many things that didn't follow what we all thought of as "the rules."

"Be careful." I squeezed Alek's arm. "I'll try not to crash your truck."

9

I realized that Alek's truck was almost out of gas, so I detoured past the B&B turnoff and headed into town. I grabbed a change of clothes from my house and checked on the store, taping up a note saying we were closed for the weekend. I hoped my few regulars would forgive me. The wards on both apartment and shop were intact and undisturbed. Then I filled Alek's tank, amazed at how much fuel fit in it as opposed to my little econo vehicle, and headed back.

I hadn't realized how worried I'd still been until I heard her laughing and teasing Max as I entered the Henhouse. Harper was awake and sitting up.

I took a moment to check my wards, though they'd done a fat lot of good against the ninja assassin. Still, it made me feel slightly better, though that could have been the feel of my magic rushing through me. All the sleep I'd gotten had done a decent job of fighting back the exhaustion, my nap with Alek refreshing me more than I realized.

If the assassin returned here tonight, I would be ready. I had an idea or three about how to deal with him. No more hesitation.

Harper and Max were playing the Electronic Talking Battleship with an original board, a relic from the late eighties. The electronics still worked, little pings and crash noises coming through the speaker.

"Hey," Harper said as I came in and settled into the chair I'd slept in the night before. "Where's your handsome half?"

"Out," I said. I didn't know what to tell her.

"Still riding the secrets train, I see," she said, making a face.

"Glad you are feeling better," I said.

"She's fine. She's just lapping up the attention." Max entered a number and a letter. A crashing noise rang out from the Battleship board.

"Fuck, you sank my battleship." Harper stuck her tongue out.

Max laughed and then straightened as his phone buzzed loudly in his pocket. He pulled it out, flicked the screen, and then handed it to me. There was a text from Alek, telling me he was going to meet with Justice Eva to interview alphas and work on the case.

"There's a second Justice in town?" Max asked.

"Wait, what? Who?" Harper set the gameboard aside with a wince.

"Some woman, a wolf, named Eva Phillips. She's kind of a bitch. Oh, and she told Sheriff Lee and some of the Wylde pack what I am. So I give it a day or two at most before every supernatural in town knows. Kickass, eh?" I pulled my knees up, tucking my feet under me, staring at the text message on the phone.

Phone. Oh, right. "Max, can I check my messages on this thing?" I asked.

"Sure, if you know how to work it, and you know your box number and password."

"I don't know. I'm so ancient I might have forgotten." I smiled at him. "I touch this screen thing here, right?"

"Okay, okay," he said, putting up his hands in surrender. "I could have worded that better. You are as bad as Lea."

"That's not my name," Harper said. "Don't make me kick your ass."

"Like you could catch me right now, gimpy."

"Guys," I said. "I'm trying to check a message here?"

They continued making silly faces at each other as they cleared the Battleship board and began a new game.

I had one message, sent this morning at seven fifty am.

"Jade Crow? This is Liam Wulfson. Alek gave me your number. He said if we found the car to call you, since he wasn't expecting to be in town. He said you could help and would want to see it. I'm out at the…" He paused. After a breath he called out, "Justice!" and I heard a woman's voice answer, followed by a shuffling noise and a crack that sounded like a gunshot. Then the message ended.

Fuck.

I played it again. And again. Each time hearing the same thing. Him telling me they found the car. Him calling out "Justice" and then the sound of a gun. Adrenaline hit me as I realized that Alek was going to meet with Eva. I dropped the phone as I jumped up and had to scrabble for it under the bed.

I called Alek back but his phone went straight to voicemail. I checked the text message and it was timed stamped over twenty minutes before I'd seen it.

"Jade?" Max and Harper looked at me, alarm in their faces.

"Why didn't you see this before?" I yelled at Max, shoving the phone in his face. "Why is it here twenty minutes after it was sent?" Why did I stop for gas? For clothes? How much time had I wasted? Would she hurt Alek?

"Jade!" Rosie came into the room, flour from the bread she had been kneading floating off her hands and arms. "Stop yelling."

I stopped and looked at her, shaking. The twins and Junebug appeared in the doorway behind her, all my friends watching me for an explanation.

"The Justice," I said. "The woman. I think she killed Liam."

"Liam? Like Wulf's son Liam?" Rosie said, her hands twisting in her apron.

"Yes. I have to find him. Alek is going to meet her." I threw the phone at Max and pulled Alek's keys from my pocket. I could trace these—they were his; he kept them on him all the time.

Except I needed them to drive. No, wait. Someone else could drive me. I looked desperately at Levi over Rosie's shoulder.

"Can you drive? I have to track Alek. We have to save him."

"Go," Junebug said. She and Ezee stepped aside as I rushed out the door, Levi at my heels.

Levi's Honda Civic didn't look like a speedy car, but he had clearly made some aftermarket modifications to it. We gunned down the drive and out onto the road. I poured magic into the keys, visualizing Alek, his smell, the feel of him. The link was strong, an undeniable pull and a thick silvery thread stretching out into the dark.

I wasn't that surprised when it took us back to the quarry.

"She has a gun," I told Levi as he cut the lights and stopped the car just off the highway. We were going to walk in on foot, just in case.

He nodded and shifted to his animal form. Wolverines look somewhat like bears, but cuter. Until they open their mouths or reveal their claws. Then they are kind of fucking scary. Wolverines the size of a Doberman? Scarier. Levi slipped silently into the shadows, leaving me alone on the track.

I ran. Eva would be able to hear me coming no matter what I did, so I gave up stealth in favor of shields and speed.

Mental note: definitely taking up running if I lived through the night. My lungs and legs burned. My pool exertions were clearly not enough to counter my sedentary, geeky lifestyle.

Alek was ahead, his keys yanking me toward him with the power of a rare-earth magnet. I dropped the tracking spell and stuffed his keys in my pocket, stopping only long enough to pull Samir's knife from its sheath at my ankle. If this thing could hurt an Undying, I figured it could really fuck up a shifter.

I threw light out ahead of me, not trusting just the moonlight, though the rising moon was nearly full. Soft purple light spread across the quarry like bioluminescent graffiti. Just beyond where we'd parked the night before, I saw Alek.

He was on the ground, not moving, looking like an apparition in the ghostly mix of silver moonlight and violet spell light. A furry body streaked toward him and I almost blasted it off the stones. Then I recognized Levi's shape as he shifted from wolverine to man and bent over Alek's body.

I skidded to a stop and fell to my knees on the rocks, my hands reaching for Alek, feeling for a pulse. He was warm to my touch, his chest still rising and falling. I looked up, looked around.

"No one around that I can smell or hear," Levi said. "There is something on him though, something wrong with his smell. And I smell blood." He touched Alek's collar where a smear of greenish fluid had stained his grey undershirt.

I saw a stain along Alek's side and lifted his arm. Blood soaked his side and the back of his shirt. Cursing, we turned him carefully and found the bullet wound. Bitch had shot him in the back.

"Alek," I said, shaking him. "Alek, you have to wake up." I knew what the smear was before I found the puncture mark in the side of his neck, near where it joined the shoulder.

"We have to get him to Vivian," I said. "He's been poisoned."

"Poisoned?" Levi shook his head. "But—"

"Don't fucking argue. This is how Dorrie died. We don't have time."

"Dorrie is dead?"

"Levi! Please." I tried to lift Alek, but couldn't even get his torso off the ground.

"I've got him," Levi said. He lifted Alek as though the man weighed only a hundred pounds, but Alek's body was long and awkward. I grabbed his feet and we managed to carry him to the boulders. Levi sprinted down the road and brought his car as close as he could get it, while I hovered over Alek, nervously watching the shadows of the quarry for movement. Getting him stuffed into the small vehicle was another exercise in frustration. Everything was taking too long.

Vivian lived above her practice, and my shouts and banging on her back door brought her downstairs quickly.

The three of us managed to get Alek inside, but his body wasn't going to fit on an exam table, so Vivian had us take him into her office. There was a narrow couch there along one wall, but it was far too short and cramped for him to fit, so we laid him on the floor. She listened to his heart, checked the puncture wound, and pressed a bandage to the bullet wound in his back. Then she checked his reflexes, and poked and prodded him while I tried not to chew off all my fingernails or blow the place up with the rage and magic boiling inside me.

"We can try adrenaline straight to his heart," she said finally, looking up at me. "If we can rouse him, enough that he can shift, he might stand a chance."

"Do it," I said. I remembered her description of the poison. How it was eating away at his organs, his heart. I grasped my talisman and prayed to the Universe not to take him. I had just gotten him back. He couldn't die like this. It wasn't fair. It wasn't right.

She left and came back with a long-needled syringe that looked like something out of *Pulp Fiction*, partially filled with greenish liquid. Deftly she knelt over Alek and sliced his shirt open. With a murmured prayer of her own, she jammed the needle into his heart, depressing the plunger.

We all held our breaths. The silence was complete, only the sound of Alek's ragged breathing, like the ticking of an old, erratic clock, breaking our vigil.

Nothing. His eyelids didn't even flutter.

"More," I said.

Vivian shook her head. "That's all I had. That stuff is highly regulated."

"No," I said. "I won't accept this. Get out." I needed them out, needed time and space to think, to figure this out. I had power. Lots and lots of fucking power. What was poison against a motherfucking sorceress?

"Jade," Levi said, touching my shaking shoulders with gentle hands.

"Out," I said. Whatever he saw in my face convinced him it was in his best interest to go.

They left me alone with Alek. I placed my hands on his chest, trying to send my magic into him, visualizing the poison as a foreign agent, as a thing that could be burned out and destroyed.

For a moment it felt like his body responded; his breathing changed, grew steadier beneath my palms. I sank into him with my consciousness and my heartbeat changed, turning erratic and painful. My lungs burned and a headache to end all headaches speared me between the eyes. I was dying.

I lashed out with magic, recoiling from the acid eating away at me. Recoiling back into my own body. Bile rose in my throat and I vomited blood, barely turning my head to the side in time to avoid splashing Alek's chest.

The headache continued but my heart steadied and the feeling of my insides burning away faded.

That was not the way to heal someone with magic, apparently.

"Alek," I said. "Tell me how to do this."

No answer.

So much power, and here I was, helpless again. I got up, took a folded throw blanket from the narrow couch, and spread it over him. I found tissues and cleaned up my vomit as best I could before lying down next to Alek, pressing myself against him. His heart was still beating. He was still fighting.

I touched the puncture wound on his neck, imagined Eva luring Alek out to the quarry. What would she have told him? How did he not see her lies? I guessed that she would be very good at not quite lying. Did she have others helping her? No way to tell. Alek would have been vulnerable anyway. He didn't like her, perhaps didn't even trust her, but she was a Justice. They had both been sent by the Council. He would trust in that. Let her get close enough to shoot him in the back. To drive the poison needle into his flesh.

Tears choked my throat, burned my eyes. That bitch was going to die. I wanted to go find her, but I couldn't bring myself to leave him. The least I could do was stay, keep trying with my magic to heal him. I pressed more power into him, not sinking into him with my mind but just letting magic flow into him. But I might as well have been channeling at a rock. A rock would have absorbed the magic better, probably.

Sorcerers can't eat shifter hearts. They have a level of immunity to most kinds of magic and their power can't transfer. The same thing that protected shifters from sorcery was preventing me now from helping him. The best I could do was kill him more quickly. I smashed that thought to pieces as I rubbed the tears from my eyes.

The door creaked open and Levi poked his head in, one hand on the door as though ready to flee and close it behind him if I snapped at him again.

"Jade," he said softly. "Can we help?"

"No," I said. "No one can." Then I froze, a memory rising in me. Alek and Carlos roaring and crows falling from the sky, changing back to their human forms.

"Wait," I said. "If he shifts, could he heal? Ask Vivian."

"Yes," she said, looking in at me from under Levi's arm. "I think he is strong enough. But he can't shift if he doesn't wake up. I think there is too much damage."

"But what if someone made him shift?" I asked.

"No one can force a shift on another," Levi said.

"I've seen it. I watched Alek make crow shifters come back to human."

Levi looked down at Vivian and they both shook their heads. "Perhaps that is a power the Council grants. I've never heard of such a thing, but Justices are special."

"So we'd need a Justice?" I asked, defeat stabbing the hope in my heart to death. "I thought it might be an alpha thing."

"No," Vivian said.

The only Justice I had access to wouldn't do it, I was sure of that. For a moment I indulged in a very violent fantasy of hunting her down and forcing her to make Alek shift, but I knew from the tiny bit of logic left in me that she would never cave. Eva had too much at stake if she was willing to kill another Justice.

"The Council, what about them?" I was grasping at very tiny straws but any glimmer of a chance...

"They do not directly interfere. We may as well ask Jesus Christ to intercede," Levi said, a bitter note in his voice. I wondered at it but shoved the questions aside.

"Jade," Vivian said. She licked her lips and glanced up at Levi again. "The Justice is strong. He's suffering. He will take a long time to die. That isn't right."

"No," I whispered. "It isn't. Just...give me a few minutes. Let me say goodbye."

My real words were unspoken. *Give me time to think. Give me time to figure out how to cheat my own personal hell, my own Kobayashi Maru.*

She nodded, and they left me alone with him again.

My magic was no good, not the way I wanted to use it. Bernard Barnes had been able to affect shifters with his magic. I didn't want to think about the evil warlock who had nearly killed my friends, who had used dark rituals to bind shifters into their animal forms and turned them into living magic batteries for his use.

I hated touching his memories. The last time I had, I had done so quickly, using Bernie's knowledge to lock Sky Heart into his human form, preventing him from fleeing Not Afraid's wrath. I had been so full of rage, my heart full of images of death, that delving into Bernie's power inside me hadn't fazed me then. It had barely registered. Yet in so doing, in using Bernie's knowledge, I had brought about the death of my father. Or at least, the man I'd thought was my father.

Bernie had been a serial killer. His psyche, and therefore his memories, were sick, full of things I didn't want to see or experience, twisted experiments, a full spectrum of human suffering and death. A PowerPoint presentation in full sensory detail on how awful one being can treat another.

But somewhere in that knowledge could be my answer. If Bernie could lock a shifter into animal shape, he could force a shift. He had laid a magical trap that had nearly forced my friends to turn on each other, had pushed them to shift. Somewhere in the hellish miasma of his memories, there might be a way to save Alek.

I had to look.

I slipped my hands around Alek's limp fingers, closed my eyes, and sank down into my own mind.

But the first memory that came wasn't Bernie's. It was my own.

"Come on in, Jess, I won't bite," Ji-hoon says. He sits at his drafting table, pen in hand. There is ink on his lip where he chews the pen nub while inking.

I slip into the room. I'm in trouble, I think. I lit a boy's hair on fire with my mind. Pretty sure that was going to be the final straw. I don't want to go back onto the street but at least I am a couple years older now. Stronger.

"I'm sorry," I whisper. "I lost control."

"That boy called you some pretty awful names?" Ji-hoon has his own kind of magic, like how he always knows things. I know that the school called him, so it isn't really magic, but something in his face calms me. He's not mad.

It's weird.

"I know that is no excuse," I say, trying to show how mature I am. How I can take responsibility for my actions.

"*The school can't prove you did it, since all witnesses say you were standing ten feet away,*" he says. "*Relax.*"

"*But I hurt someone.*"

"*And you feel terrible about it, even though he was totally being an asshole. That's good. The fire only burned his hair, from what the principal told me. So you stopped yourself, put it out, right?*" He smiles at me and goes back to inking, putting clean black lines over his sketches, bringing the comic to life.

"*I did, but…I don't feel good. I feel like a freak, like a bigger asshole than he was.*" Now I'm a little mad. I want him to tell me I'm a bad person. This power inside me, it isn't normal. I couldn't be like my real family, and now I'm not like my new one, either. I'm a freak.

"*You don't feel good because you* are *good,*" Ji-hoon says. "*Your magic is just magic, Jess. It is like lightning or the ocean. A part of the world. It can be harnessed and used for good or ill. But it just is. You choose. Today you chose to hurt. Now you know what that feels like. Tomorrow you can choose differently.*"

"*My magic hurt him,*" I say.

"*No,*" he says. "*You hurt him. Your magic is no more to blame for that than my pen is for creating this line.*"

The memory faded and I sank deeper, cursing at my subconscious. It hurt to see Ji-hoon, even in my memories. I had buried that family, hiding them so I wouldn't dream, wouldn't hurt. Parts of myself felt like they were waking up now. Parts I wasn't sure I wanted to see again, things I didn't want to feel.

I shoved that away, too.

Bernard Barnes. Ah. There he was. Brown, thinning hair. Watery blue eyes. Pudgy, pale body. His memories started to flood me but I scoured through them, burning away the images, the impressions. Setting fire to every crime, every murder, every pain perpetrated by his choices, his use of the power he gained. I faced the deaths in my memories and rejected them. Not my actions, not my choices. They had no power over me, no more than death on a TV screen would.

I did not want those things, but I faced them unflinching. For Alek. For myself. What I was and who I was, as Ji-hoon had pointed out when I was way too young to listen, was up to me. My choices. Not Bernie's, nor that boy who so long ago had looked at my brown skin and called me names.

I faced the pain and suffering Bernie had wrought and set it alight in my mind. I sought only his knowledge, the bright core of what he had learned. I wanted the tool, not its wielder. Ji-hoon was right. Power was power.

There, amidst the coals in my psyche, I found the knowledge I wanted. A ritual inscribed in an ancient book, a trap to set for men who could change their shape, forcing them from man to beast.

I am a sorceress. I have no need of ritual to raise power. I had Bernie's power, now scrubbed clean and joined with my own. Just power. Just magic. A tool, a means to whatever end I wanted.

Balancing the scales, perhaps, a little more in favor of good. Not undoing what Bernie had done to gain such knowledge, not justifying it, but perhaps adding my own feather to the opposite side. Bernie had chosen to use the knowledge to bring death. I chose life.

I swam up to consciousness with the bit of knowledge clutched in my mental fist like a pearl. Alek still breathed beside me, his heartbeat fainter now. I pressed my magic into my newfound knowledge, following the unfamiliar patterns and shapes of the ritual with my mind, painting a circle around us in golden light. Magic oozed from me, filling each line as I drew it.

"Alek," I whispered, pouring my will into the circle. "Be a tiger."

Then the circle snapped into place and the hand I held became a paw, too big for my hands to encompass. The man struggling to live beside me became a huge white tiger, his body shoving aside the desk with his weight.

His heart steadied. His breathing evened out. He slept.

Levi and Vivian must have heard me shout with joy as I let the circle fade away. I didn't know what words were coming from my mouth, which languages I spoke to them in. I clung to his paw and rubbed my cheek on his rough fur.

Vivian checked his vitals, drawing blood. She left, but after a few minutes she returned, her face full of awe. When she looked at me, there was a shadow of fear in her eyes. "His body is untainted by poison. He will sleep for a while, I think, while his other self fights the poison, but I think he is strong enough to purge it. The twilight is a powerful place."

"Twilight?" I said.

"Nothing to do with the book," Levi said as he knelt beside me, touching Alek's fur as though to reassure himself that the tiger was real. "It's what some of us call the place where our non-physical self lives. Ezee calls it the Cave, after Plato's work."

His dark eyes met mine, and I was relieved to see no fear in them. Of course, he had known for months what I was. Vivian, not so much. I had a feeling my days of living anonymously as just another low-power witch in a town full of supernaturals were about to be a distant memory after the events of this weekend.

That would be a bridge I'd fireball when I came to it.

"Can we move him?" I asked.

"It's safe to move him," Vivian said with a wan smile. "But I am not sure we are physically capable of getting him out of here."

"I'd like to try," I said. "I'd rather have him at the Henhouse than here. You, too, Vivian. If Eva figures out he didn't die in the quarry, she might come here."

"Eva? The other Justice?" Vivian looked like she might faint. Her face got splotchy and she took a couple of deep breaths.

In my rage and pain I'd forgotten to mention who had shot and poisoned him, and apparently Levi hadn't mentioned it either. Oops.

"Yeah," I said. "I'm pretty sure she's the one killing people and framing wolves. I think she wants the Peace to fall apart. Just wish I knew why."

None of us had answers for that, alas. Yet.

Levi called Ezee and Max. Turned out that three gamers who all played *Tetris* could figure how to move a tiger out of a small room and into a truck. The whole four people with preternatural strength thing helped, of course. We only had to remove two doors to do it.

I rode in the back with Alek, my cheek pressed to his chest, listening to his heart. In my own heart, the joy of knowing he would survive was fading. In its place rage simmered. White heat flowed through my veins, my magic responding to my mood.

As soon as I was sure Alek would live, as soon as he was okay, I was going to balance the scales another way. I was going to find Eva, and this time, I was going to choose murder.

Using a lot of shifter strength and a heavy-duty canvas tarp, we managed to get Alek into the Henhouse and onto a makeshift pallet of quilts in the formal living room. I hovered as they moved him, not wanting him out of my sight. He breathed easily, his heart steady when I pressed my face against his chest.

"He'll live, I promise," Vivian said to me. The awe was still in her eyes.

"I know," I said, still pressed against his fur.

Everyone crowded into the living room, asking questions in low voices. Rosie shushed them and handed me a warm washcloth. She was wise enough to realize I wasn't going to leave Alek's side until he woke up, until I heard from his own lips that he was going to survive. I must have looked a mess. My shirt was stained with Alek's blood and covered in long white tiger hairs. My hands had blood under the nails and streaks of dust and dirt going up my arms. I couldn't imagine what my face looked like. Or my hair.

"Eva did this," I said as I handed back a much grimier washcloth to Rosie with a nod of thanks.

"The Justice?" Rosie asked. The others echoed her, their faces full of disbelief.

"I believer her," Max said. He looked at me with unhappy eyes.

"I, too, believe her," Harper said. She came into the room, a quilt wrapped around her. Her normally pale face was even whiter, but she moved easily and without evidence of pain. "I heard Liam's message. Max and I listened to it after you left."

"She is a Justice," Junebug said. "How could she kill like that? Attack another Justice?"

"It's worse than that," I said and I told them everything. About the Lansings, about the poison, the set-up with Dorrie's body.

Stunned silence followed my story.

"But, the Council—" Ezee started to say.

"Fuck the Council," Levi said. "They pick and choose. You know that, Ezekiel. Where were they, where were their Justices when we needed them? When Mama needed them?"

"Levi," Junebug and Ezee both cried out, looking at him.

Levi's eyes were shiny with pain and unshed tears. "I'm sorry," he said as he took a deep breath. "I...this situation, it's too hard. But I believe Jade. The Justices are not infallible, the Council is not infallible, and I think it will only get more of us hurt to continue believing such things."

"All right," Rosie said softly. "If this Eva woman is corrupt, why is she doing this? Why now?"

"I have a guess," Vivian said. She was curled on the overstuffed couch, her legs tucked up against her chest, her arms wrapped around them. "You are all too young to remember how it was before the Peace. You are not wolves. You do not understand. I was a child then, but it was still dangerous to be without pack. My mother moved us around, unwelcome because she was an alpha, but she had no desire to run a pack. An unmarried woman, traveling with a small child, was crazy in those days. There was little work, and I won't speak of the work she *could* get. We were always in danger. From other wolves. From humans."

She paused and looked down at Alek's huge, slumbering form. "There was too much fighting among wolves; too many alphas and not enough pack. Stories started being told around human campfires, in human brothers and taverns, of wolves the size of ponies, of men who changed shape and howled at the moon. Men were dying. Men disappearing. Then the Council of Nine sent their Justices to America and the shifters of the new world learned the power of the Council. They learned to fear. Back then a Justice only showed up when someone was slated to die—they were executioners as much as judges, killers as much as protectors."

I brushed my hand over Alek's fur. He couldn't hear this story, lost as he was in healing sleep, but I knew he would agree with Vivian. He would be thinking that the Justices were killers still. I recalled his face, his eyes piercing and earnest as he told me that this is who he was, what he was.

"Eva was one of those Justices," I said. Alek had told me as much.

"Yes. She put down the bloodiest of the packs, killed their alphas as examples of what the Council would do. She formed her own pack, a group of bloody hunters she called her Hands of Justice. If it hadn't been for Wulf, who knows how long the killings would have gone on. My mother and I lived on the edge of Wulf's territory by that time. He gathered alpha wolves from all over the new territories and the original States, and they pledged in blood on the sword of his father to keep the Peace, to allow wolves to live within their territory, to allow alphas to be pack brothers and sisters. Because all territory would be his territory. All alphas subservient to the alpha of alphas. He fought and defeated all challengers for weeks, until they had submitted, until they had signed."

"What about the Bitteroot pack?" I asked, thinking of what the wolves had said as we'd stood by Liam's body.

Vivian shook her head. "Aurelio, who is called Softpaw now, refused to sign. He refused to challenge Wulf as well. Instead he left, taking his pack. They live as wolves. Perhaps they thought the Peace a concern for those of us who walk on two legs."

"And Eva?" Harper asked.

"She was one of three Justices who witnessed the Peace. My mother told me a Justice tried to challenge Wulf, but that she was sent away by the other two. I had never met Eva before yesterday, but the story fits together now."

Furniture creaked as everyone settled back, and a chorus of held breaths released sighed around the living room.

"So she wants to be the alpha of alphas?" I speculated.

"Or she wants more chaos, for the wolf packs to fight again, so that she can bring her own version of justice down," Levi said.

"I guess that fits with what Alek said about her," I said. "He said she liked to execute first and ask questions never." It fit somewhat too with the whole "trying to set up wolves to look like killers of the humans in Wylde." A massive wolf hunt and lots of human attention would cause huge risk to the shifter population and to their secrecy. The Council would send a Justice. Eva clearly believed it would be her.

I just wanted to know how the Council hadn't seen this coming. If they were really some kind of gods, why wasn't there an army of Justices here to stop Eva? Why only Alek, and why hadn't they warned him?

"What are we going to do?" Ezee asked.

"We? Nothing," I said firmly. "I'm going to wait until Alek wakes up, then I'm going to go kill me a wolf bitch."

"But she's a Justice," Junebug said.

"She's evil," I said. Didn't get much more evil in my book than murdering a family, killing and framing an innocent woman, and then killing anyone who got in your way. Oh, and the fact that she shot and poisoned my lover was like the deserves-to-die-horribly cherry topping on a giant I-will-smite-you sundae.

"But the Council—what if they come after you? She is still a Justice," Harper said.

"Fuck the Council," I said, smiling grimly at Levi as he nodded. "What's one more thing trying to fuck up my life, right?"

"We have to warn the alphas. At least call Sheriff Lee and whoever is in charge at the Den now." Max had his phone out.

"Freyda," I said, remembering Liam's sister. She had seemed smart and steady. I just hoped she would believe us. "Will they believe us?"

"I don't know, but warning can't hurt," Ezee said. He pulled out his phone as well.

"Straight to voicemail at the Den," Max said. "Says they are closed this week and to leave a message."

Vivian got up and retrieved her coat, getting her own phone out. She tried calling Henry, then Freyda directly. Every call went to voicemail.

"Sheriff Lee is busy," Ezee said. "So dispatch tells me. They said if it is an emergency to call nine-one-one."

"No," I said. "That would get humans responding; too many problems with that."

"They are holding vigil tonight," Vivian said. "They will inter Wulf's body at dawn in the Great Hall. Then the challenges will start and go until there is only one alpha. It was likely to have been Liam. I am not sure who is likely now. At moonrise they will pledge their blood to the sword and reaffirm the Peace."

"So we've got until dawn or maybe later even before things get really hoary," I said. "Will Alek wake up by then?" *Please, Universe, let him wake up by then.*

"He might," Vivian said. She stared at her phone and then sighed, shutting it off.

I realized everyone was looking at me, waiting. I felt like the game master of my own life suddenly, caught without the notes or my dice, woefully unprepared. I didn't even know what system we were playing.

"You all have seen the evidence for yourselves and yet find it hard to believe Eva could do these things. If we try to go warn them tonight, we'll be outsiders, interrupting and accusing a Justice with no way to prove what we're saying," I said, thinking aloud. "We need Alek. I don't see a way to salvage the Peace and stop Eva without him." I wanted to go after her myself, as soon as possible, but I knew that just killing her would make things worse for my friends, for Alek. For a lot of shifters, probably.

It wasn't what Alek would want. Balancing the scales. Killing, but only to save as many lives as possible.

"We stay here, we stay alert, and we wait for Alek to wake," I said. It was something like a plan, at least. "At dawn we will go and try to warn the wolves and stop Eva."

"And if he doesn't wake by dawn?" Harper said, worried green eyes focused on the huge sleeping tiger at my side.

"I'll storm the castle and do shit the hard way." My magic responded to my anger, rising in me until my normally light brown skin glowed pearl and violet for a moment. It felt like there was a switch inside of me now, waiting to be flipped. I was ready to stop reacting, ready to stop defending.

Ready to kill.

None of us slept much that night. Levi and Ezee and Rosie traded off watching out a crack in the front blinds and sitting with the rifle. People came and went from the living room, but mostly my friends left me alone with Alek. Rosie brought me a hot cup of sweet orange tea at some point. I stayed seated on the floor beside my tiger, watching him breathe.

I must have dozed off at some point. A damp nose against my neck woke me. Wolf. She walked to the window as though she could see through the curtains, her lips peeling back from teeth as long as my fingers in a silent snarl.

An odd hum buzzed in my ears and my skin tingled. My wards. Something or someone was moving out there. I sent my awareness spiraling out into the circles I had placed around the Henhouse. One, two, then others. At least six bodies out there, not human.

So not the assassin. I was willing to bet they were shifters, wolves. But friend or foe? Looking at Wolf's snarling face, I assumed foe.

"Where have you been?" I whispered to her. "You could have warned me about Eva a little sooner." It was useless to complain. Wolf had her own priorities and ideas about things. Eva was of the physical world mostly, not a threat that Wolf could protect me against. I guess, technically, not one she needed to, since Eva couldn't kill me. Still, I couldn't help feel a little warning would have been nice. She was warning me now, after all.

Next to me, Alek moved. His huge head lifted and his eyes opened. He twisted, scrabbling in the quilts, pulling his legs beneath him, his lips coming back in a snarl. Then recognition bloomed in his pale eyes and he shifted to human.

"Jade," he said with a wince. His shirt was torn and bloody, with the bandage still on his back.

"Should you shift yet?" I said as he pulled the ruin of his shirt off and contorted to rip free the bandage.

"The poison is gone," he said. "I'll live."

I crawled onto the quilts and ran my fingers over the bullet wound in his back. Only a pink scar remained. He pulled me into his lap and we clung to each other for a long moment.

"I heard you," he said. "In my mind, I heard you calling to me, telling me to shift. I felt you send me into the twilight."

"You're welcome," I said, smiling against his chest.

He pulled away from me, looking down into my eyes. "It was Eva," he said.

"We know. Liam left me a message and I heard her kill him."

"How did you find me?" he asked, and then smiled ruefully. "Ah, let me guess. Magic."

"Alek! Alek's awake!" Max stopped at the edge of the carpet and started yelling, a huge grin on his face.

Everyone came running to the living room. Alek held on to me as he quickly answered their questions, confirming for all of them that Eva had really gone rogue. I was okay with that, not wanting to break contact with him, not trusting yet that he was okay. The image of him dying, burning up on the inside, was too fresh.

Wolf snarled again, still staring out the window, and I remembered the bodies, my wards. Shit.

"There's people outside," I said. "Six or so I think. Shifters is my guess."

"Fuck," Harper said.

"It is nearly dawn," Vivian said.

"Is Eva out there?" Alek asked me. "Can you tell?"

I shook my head. "I don't think so, but I can't tell. All I know is six non-humans are just inside the edge of the wards. They rang the alarm, basically."

"So they are staying in the treeline, out of sight. Show me where," Rosie said.

I reluctantly got up and went into the dining room, grabbing a piece of notepaper off the sideboard. Harper handed me a pen, and Alek followed, standing over me as I sat at the table and drew a rough diagram of the property, marking out where I felt the bodies.

"So, two at the back door, four covering the front and angles there. I think they are here to keep us inside. Pinned down." Alek's eyes narrowed.

"She's afraid of us showing up and ruining her party," Harper said.

"She knows I'm a sorceress," I said. "She should be afraid. I'm going to kill her."

"No," Alek said. "You are not."

I twisted in the chair and glared up at him. "Did you just say what I think you said?"

"She will die," Alek said. His tone softened but held a dangerous, deadly edge. It made me think of forest shadows and screaming prey. "I will bring her to justice."

I almost argued. Alek wasn't full strength; he had nearly died only hours before. His face convinced me to shut up. Eva had betrayed more than Alek and the shifters she had killed. She had abused and betrayed her position as Justice. Betrayed her gods. This was Justice business, and I understood Alek's need to balance the scales. I understood, too, that a Justice killing the rogue Justice might be necessary to salvage their reputations.

And hey, if it kept his Council from wanting to kill me in retribution, I was okay with that as well.

"I'm coming with you," I said. He might be able to take on Eva, but I was going to make sure he got to her in one piece, and be there to lend my power if needed.

That was when the wolves watching the house got bored and started shooting at the cars.

"They shot my car," Levi snarled as he peeked out the front blinds. He looked ready to shift and go lay some serious wolverine rage down on them.

"They shot all the cars," Ezee said. "Sounds like automatic fire, too."

"Where did they get automatics?" Vivian asked. "Used to be we solved our problems with tooth and claw." Her disapproval was almost funny in its school marm way.

"It's 'Murica, fuck yeah," Max said with an eye roll.

I looked through the blinds. The sun was rising. False dawn tinged the horizon the color of fresh meat and cast a hazy shroud over the tree line.

"I could go out there," I said. "Bullets won't kill me. I think I can shield against them."

"Hold up there, Rambo," Harper said. "They might not kill you, but they won't do you any favors, either. How are you going to stop Eva if you burn yourself out trying to stop bullets?"

Furball had a point. I sighed, frustrated.

"Can you shield enough to distract the two in back?" Junebug asked me.

Two people shooting at me was better than four. I nodded. "True, there are fewer out there. Maybe we can break out and circle around, take the others by surprise."

"You want to sneak up on shifters? Who have machine guns?" Rosie pursed her lips, clearly not on board with anyone going outside and getting shot at.

"They can't use the guns if they aren't human," Alek said. The killing look was back on his face, his eyes glacially cold and scary.

I remembered him forcing the crows in my former tribe to shift. "How close do you have to be?"

"They only need to hear me," he said.

"You can make them shift?" Ezee asked.

I saw Vivian and Levi both glance at me before looking back at Alek. I'd told those two as much.

Alek inclined his head slightly, a grim smile touching his lips. "I am a Justice of the Council of Nine," he said softly. "They will rue this day."

"Good," Junebug said. She brushed her hands over her skirt and took a deep breath, glancing at Levi. "Distract them, and I will fly out of here. You will need a car to get to the Den. I can fly to the shop and bring one. Just make sure they are gone before I return."

"What? No," Levi said. "It isn't safe."

"Don't you lecture me about safe," she hissed at him. I could almost envision her feathers ruffling as her eyes widened and her shoulders hunched up. "You run around with your brother and your friends, getting yourself nearly killed by a warlock. You are ready even now to run out there and fight a pack of wolves. I am your wife, Levi, not a sweet little princess sitting helpless waiting for her knight to come home. Let me help."

"Dude," Ezee murmured with a smile, "I think your princess is in another castle."

"Shut up," Levi said to his twin. He moved away from the window and wrapped his arms around Junebug. "All right," he murmured into her hair. "Bring the Mustang. We'll have them cleared out."

I pulled my magic around me like a cloak, hardening it until I felt encased in stone. I hoped it was enough.

Opening the back door just enough to slip through, I dashed out and across the porch, diving down the steps. Gunfire crackled from the trees at the back of the house. Pieces of the porch splintered as bullets chunked into the wood. I was definitely going to dig into my savings and buy Rosie some serious home repairs after this weekend.

I dodged behind a low brick flowerbed. Poking my head over it, I threw bolts of white light at the trees fifty yards or so out. That was where gunfire had originated. The light was meant to blind them in the dim light, distract. Give Alek a chance to get out the door if we determined the wolves were close enough for his magic to take effect. And to give Junebug a chance to fly from an upper window.

Behind me, a coughing roar rang out, vibrating with power. Alek.

Tiger-Alek stood on the porch, half through the rear door. I climbed to my feet, holding my shield in place. No one shot at me.

Still roaring, tiger-Alek sprang down from the porch and stalked toward the woods. Ezee, Levi, and, surprisingly, Vivian had agreed to handle the four wolves in front. They were not immune to Alek's power, so everyone except me was currently furry. Rosie had forbidden Max and Harper from fighting, pointing out that Max was only fifteen and Harper was still hurt. She'd threatened to lock them in a closet if they didn't agree and I didn't think she was bluffing.

Two large wolves hurtled from the trees and sprang at Alek. He snapped one wolf's neck with a bat of a huge paw, and spun, catching the other in the shoulder and flinging it back.

The wolf twisted in midair and scrabbled to its feet, snarling. I gathered power, ready to blast it, but Alek sprang before I could do anything. His mouth closed on the hapless wolf's throat, and blood spurted, staining tiger-Alek's white fur. He threw the body down and resumed roaring as he ran for the front of the property.

I gulped in a deep breath, staring at the dead wolves. It was one thing to say you were ready to accept killing, to know that your lover killed people as part of who he was, as part of his job. It was another thing to face it, to see the sheer power and violence right in front of me.

They did this to themselves, I told myself. They shot at us. They chose Eva's side. They chose wrong.

I gave myself a mental shake and ran after Alek.

The fighting had spilled out of the woods. Wolverine-Levi tangled with a huge white wolf, fur and blood flying as they engaged and came apart. A smaller, red-furred wolf who I guessed was Vivian circled a bigger grey wolf, driving it back toward where coyote-Ezee crouched in the long grass, snarling and watching for an opening.

A third wolf leapt at Vivian, blood streaking its grey and black fur. Tiger-Alek reached the wolf before it landed, bounding across the distance in giant strides and slamming the wolf down into the grass with a sickening crunch I heard even from forty feet away.

Coyote-Ezee took advantage of the distraction of Alek's arrival and darted in, teeth ripping into the grey wolf's hamstring. Vivian leapt as the wolf twisted and yelped in pain. Her jaws closed on the bigger wolf's throat and together they went down in the grass, struggling.

A snarl and movement in my peripheral vision warned me as the fourth wolf streaked toward me from the side. I guessed that it thought that the lone human would be an easier target for its rage. I spun and lashed out with my magic, focusing it into bolts of force.

The bolts hit the wolf, sizzling in its fur and knocking it down. Shaking its body, the brown wolf leapt at me again, refusing to stay down.

Another wolf, its fur red and white, streaked in, moving with impossible speed. This one was young, lanky, and much smaller than the brown wolf. They collided and rolled away from each other, snarling and circling as they regained their feet.

Max. Dammit. Rosie hadn't locked him in a closet after all. Probably hard to do as a fox without thumbs.

The two wolves circled around me, moving with such speed that I didn't trust myself to aim true if I threw more magic at the brown one. I dropped my shield, fatigue starting to send little heralds of headache pain into my brain. Crouching, I went for Samir's knife in its ankle sheath.

It wasn't there. Cursing, I recalled it had been in my hand when we found Alek. I'd dropped it in the quarry. Fucktoast on a stick.

Something to worry about later.

Max darted toward the wolf, leaping past my legs close enough that I felt the brush of his fur. The brown wolf was quicker, more experienced. Its mouth snapped shut on Max's leg with a crunch, and Max yowled in pain.

I jumped on the brown wolf, digging my fingers into its eyes, biting an ear and ripping with my teeth.

The wolf let go of Max and whipped its body around, trying to dislodge me. I let myself fly free, spitting a piece of its ear out as I hit the grass and rolled. The wolf was impossibly fast, on top of me again before I could regain my feet.

A huge white shadow ripped the wolf away from me, leaving only a warm spray of blood behind. Alek shook the wolf as though it were a rat, and sprang onto the body as he dropped it, raking it with his back claws, rending it to shreds.

"Alek," I cried out. "It's dead. Stop."

He looked at me, mouth scarlet in the light of the rising sun, his lips peeling back in a snarl.

"Or, you know, shred away," I said, crawling to my feet without taking my eyes off his. "Knock yourself out."

An odd look came into his deadly gaze, and he coughed. I realized he was doing the tiger equivalent of laughing. I relaxed. Slightly.

Then he shifted, turning from giant, bloody tiger to tired-looking Viking in less than a blink.

"Are you okay?" he asked.

"Yeah," I said. "Max?" I turned and looked for him.

Max shifted from wolf to human, his face scrunched with pain. "Broke my leg," he said, rubbing the human limb, which appeared straight and unhurt. "I'll be okay if Mom doesn't kill me."

"I'll tell her you saved my life," I promised. "Idiot."

Ezee called out to us and we all moved back toward the house, leaving the bodies where they had fallen. Ezee and Vivian were unhurt, but Levi walked with a limp even in his human body, and cradled an arm against his side.

"I'll live," he grunted at his brother. "Stop looking at me like that. You're worse than my wife."

Alek disappeared into the trees and returned a few minutes later with an arm load of automatic weapons. "Shouldn't leave those out there," he said.

Rosie nodded and brought a sheet to wrap them in. Junebug arrived with the Mustang, gunning down the driveway with a reckless speed that rivaled Levi's driving.

"That's my princess," he said with a pained smile.

I convinced the others they had to stay at the Henhouse. Levi, Harper, and Max were in no condition to fight more, and Alek and I had no idea what we would face at the Den.

"We still don't know where the assassin is, either," I pointed out. "Alek and I can handle Eva." After seeing Alek fight, I was pretty sure Eva was worm food. Especially if I was there to make sure it stayed one on one. Turned out, dire tigers were really scary in action.

There were protests, but Alek and I were out of time. He took the keys to the Mustang and I followed him out the front door and past the bullet-riddled cars. Even his truck had eaten a magazine or two. Broken glass crunched beneath my feet.

"Have fun storming the castle," Harper called out from the porch.

I turned and waved, yelling back, "Think it will work?"

She grinned at me, obscuring the fear in her expression if not in her posture. "It would take a miracle," she said, finishing the *Princess Bride* quote.

I was fresh out of miracles, but I still had magic. And I had a Justice with me. It would have to be enough.

"We need to make a detour," I told Alek as we drove away from the Henhouse. "I left Samir's knife in the quarry." The knife was magical, a blade able to hurt things that shouldn't have been able to be hurt by physical weapons. I couldn't leave it lying around. Besides, having a weapon like that going into whatever we were driving toward at the Den wouldn't hurt.

"All right," he said. His expression was grim. His eyes met mine for a moment before returning to the road. "Are we all right?" he said softly.

I thought about the dead wolves. The blood still drying sticky on my shirt. I'd wiped the worst of it off, but I could still smell it, feel it on my skin. They had made their choices. We had made ours. All we could do was keep fighting, keep making choices, and hope the scales balanced in the end.

"Yes," I said grimly. "We're just fine."

The sun was high enough by the time we reached the quarry to fling shadows across the stones and highlight the scars and ridges in the naked rock. Alek drove the Mustang right up to the boulders.

"Keep it running," I said. "I'll be quick."

I jumped out of the car and jogged toward where Levi and I had found Alek's body the night before. There was still a dark stain on the ground from his blood and I shivered remembering his crumpled, dying body.

Samir's knife was still there. The air felt oddly still, though the scene looked undisturbed. Another shiver ran up my spine and goosebumps broke out.

A hint of smoke touched my nose as I reached the blade. Smoke and ink. Magic. Enough of a warning that I dropped flat and the first shot missed.

One of the boulders moved, resolving itself into the assassin as he raised a gun and fired again. He'd made a mistake, coming this close, choosing terrain that wouldn't burn, choosing a place where I didn't have to worry about witnesses or collateral damage.

I lashed out with magic, ripping the gun from his hands. My power raged through me. I was ready for this shit now.

I sent my magic out in a circle, throwing up a dome of force around us, boxing him in with me. He was faster than I was, in better physical shape. Clearly he knew how to fight. All advantages I didn't have.

The assassin tried to back away, drawing two more kunai as he sprang backward and slammed into my magical Thunderdome.

His breath hissed out through his teeth as he steadied himself, and his face lost its perpetually bland expression.

"Who are you?" I asked. I tied off the spell, anchoring it to the rocks. It wouldn't last forever, minutes perhaps, but I couldn't keep channeling it and shield myself as well. Or go on the attack.

"Who are you?" he asked back, his beetle-hard eyes narrowing.

I pushed my magic into a shield just over my skin, much like I had at the Henhouse before trying to attract the attention of men with machine guns. One of his kunai spun toward me and I slapped it out of the air with a glittering, shielded fist.

"Jade Crow casts harden," I muttered. "It's super effective." I tightened my grip on Samir's knife and crouched. "Only way to get out of here is to kill me," I told him. I figured saying "come at me, bro" would have been too much. Adrenaline pumped through my brain, carrying me into a high that fueled my power, made me feel like I could do anything, take on anyone. I felt giddy with magic and bloodlust.

The assassin came at me, darting in so quickly I barely got my knife up before he was slashing at me with his own blades. I felt every cut and impact on my shields, felt my power being used up, draining, each blow pushing me around, off balance. I tried to slash back, but he was far too quick, my dome giving him just enough room to maneuver on the uneven ground and circle me.

I threw bolts of force at him, recklessly spending magic. Beyond the slight shimmer of the dome, I saw Alek rush up. Saw him pause, his mouth moving. I couldn't hear his words.

Looking at Alek distracted me, and the assassin came at my back, his knife slicing into my leg, cutting through my weakening shield. White-hot pain lanced up my hip. The assassin slapped something to my back and retreated. Reaching back, I snatched the paper and flung it away from myself, dropping low as fire raged around me.

The air grew thin, breathing more difficult. My shield had cut off everything, apparently. Things to think about and refine later. Smoke filled my nose, made my eyes water. My leg gave out under me and I slashed at the dark shape as the assassin hit me again, this time taking me to the ground. I couldn't breathe. The fire had eaten all the oxygen.

He rolled me under him, trapping my legs. I looked up into his face as he sat up and pressed a kunai to my chest. His skin was blotchy, his lips turning blue. He was out of air as well.

I don't need to breathe, I told myself. *Air is optional. Remember the lessons of the pool.* I stopped breathing and focused on the magic inside myself, pouring my power out to encase the assassin in icy cold, envisioning everywhere he touched me as frozen, dead.

He tried to scream as frost rimed over him, speeding up the blade to his arm, wrapping itself around his throat, locking his limbs. Ice didn't need air. Ice was good against fire.

I pulled my arms free and smashed the dome, breaking the circle.

Air rushed in and I gasped for breath. I put Samir's knife against the assassin's throat, exhaustion making my hand shake. He was still frozen, though I felt his skin warming where he knelt on my stomach, his body starting to twitch.

I jerked the kunai out of his hand, pushing his frozen arm away from my chest, keeping my own knife against the pulse in his neck. The assassin's eyes watched me, unafraid. He was ready for death.

I wondered if he was ready for worse than death. I set my hand against his chest, felt the beating of his heart. Samir had sent him to kill me. This man had tried to kill my friends, had hurt people I loved. Plus, he had really pissed me off.

Old Jade Crow might have let him go. Months ago, I might have. He was human. A week ago, I would have merely killed him.

Today, I flipped the switch inside. No more defensive. No more playing by rules that only got people I loved hurt.

New rules.

"I'm sorry," I said softly. Then I focused my magic into my hand and ripped out the assassin's heart.

Power and knowledge surged through me as I swallowed a bite of the assassin's heart. His name was Haruki and he was forty-one years old. He hadn't lied about growing up in the Oki Shoto islands. His life flitted through my mind and I pushed it away for later examination.

I felt Alek pulling Haruki's body off me and opened my eyes, still vibrating with the new power as it mingled with my own magic, joining. Like dumping a pond into an ocean, the ripples went on for a while before fading away.

Alek helped me to my feet. I carefully sheathed Samir's knife and then tossed the remainder of Haruki's heart onto his body.

"You are injured," Alek said.

I tested my leg. The cut was already closing. "I'll live," I said. "Go to the car, I'll be there in a moment."

He studied my face for a breath and then nodded. There was no judgment in his eyes, only concern. I watched him walk away before turning back to Haruki's body.

I wiped my bloody mouth on my equally bloody teeshirt, annoyed that the blood tasted almost sweet, almost good to me. Then I crouched and closed Haruki's clouded eyes. Using his own blood and his own memories, I drew a sigil on his forehead, imbuing it with power.

"Good bye, Katayama Haruki," I said softly in Japanese, using his surname first and then his given name. Then I turned and limped to the car as his body ignited behind me, a last wave of inky heat following me. I did not look back.

13

Stonebrook Hunting Lodge, the official name of the Den, was about six miles out of town down a partially paved road that wound up a hill through pristine old-growth forest. It was a faux-castle, a hulking stone and wood building with two main wings joined by a three-story-tall great hall and flanked by squat, mostly decorative stone towers. There was only one approach to the Den; a long driveway that climbed the hill and terminated in a circular drive in front of the huge stone steps leading to the giant red doors of the great hall.

Cars filled the parking lot carved into the hill beside the Den, shining like Skittles in the morning sunlight as Alek and I stopped the Mustang at the bottom of the hill, pulling as far off to the side and into the shadow of the trees as we could.

"How many alphas are here?" I asked.

"Counting their seconds?" Alek thought for a moment as we stared up at the big stone building. Only the upper part was visible from where we were. We'd have to go farther up the drive to see the doors. "Two hundred and thirty wolves, I believe."

I wondered who the wolves we'd killed at the Henhouse had been, what pack they were with. I hoped it wasn't Wylde's pack helping betray everything their former alpha had lived for, had worked to build.

"I believe your line is 'time's up, let's do this,'" Alek said with a slight smile.

"We live through this, I'm going to make you watch that YouTube video," I said, smiling back at him. Nerves fluttered in my belly and then calmed. We would live through this, I promised myself. This was a beginning, this new start between us, and I wasn't going to give it up so easily this time.

We climbed out of the car and slipped into the woods, sticking to the trees as far up the hill as we could. The forest thinned and then terminated a couple hundred yards away from the doors. From here I could see the wide stone porch. Four figures lay prone in its surface, sunlight glinting on metal in their hands. I squinted.

Guns. Big guns. If anyone was dying inside that hall, we were too far away to hear the commotion.

"Wolves?" I asked Alek.

He took deep breaths of the air, mouth partially open as though tasting as much as smelling for their scents. He shook his head. "Human. I can't force them to shift," he added, clearly following my line of thought.

"Damn," I muttered. I reached for my magic. We were a long ways out, but I had to try to reach them. We needed inside that hall. Universe only knew what Eva was doing, what was happening in there. She had hired these men to keep anyone else from coming in. Humans with guns. Another breach of the Council's rules, I guessed, a shifter dealing with humans, using human muscle. Mercenaries. Fucked-up world.

"Wait," Alek muttered. His head swiveled and he tasted the air again.

I sensed movement in the trees behind us. Wolves.

But it was a man who emerged from the denser forest and made his way to the stand of fir we lurked within. He was about six feet tall with long, shaggy black hair that had a dramatic shock of white running through it, a thick beard, and skin a shade darker brown than my own. He smiled, his hands spread in a non-threatening gesture. Something about how he moved was almost awkward, as though he had not walked in a long time and was trying to remember how with each step. He wore only a pair of green sweatpants, no shirt or shoes.

"Justice," he said, his voice rough and gravelly. "I am Aurelio, called Softpaw, alpha of the Bitterroot pack."

Alek moved so that he was half between Aurelio and I. "That your pack in trees?" he said.

"Yes," Aurelio answered. "I have come to swear the Peace. My daughter is dead; the Justices have no hold over me any longer."

Alek and I exchanged a confused look, which Aurelio saw.

"You do not know?" he asked, the determination in his face turning to confusion. "No, I guess it has been many, many years. You are too young. One of your own, a wolf called Evaline, made me leave. My daughter killed a human trapper, and the Justice said the price for her life was for me to fight Ulfr, stop the Peace. I could not fight my friend, but I did not sign. I took my pack and we fled deep into the wilderness. But my daughter is gone. I wish to redeem my cowardice."

He said the words as though he had been rehearsing them, which I guessed he might have. It had likely been a very long time since he'd spoken with a human throat, since he'd shared words with other people.

"Good," Alek said simply. "Eva has broken the trust; she is not acting with the will of the Council."

Aurelio searched Alek's face and whatever he saw there satisfied him. "My pack is yours, Justice," he said.

"Don't suppose you know another way into the Den?" I asked.

He looked past Alek at me and shook his shaggy head. "Your mate is human? She will be in danger here," he said.

"Woah, I am not his mate," I said. "Or totally human. Check your nose."

His nostrils flared and he cocked his head. "No," he said in his rough voice. "Not human. The blood on you is, but it is not your blood."

All right. I had literally asked for that. I sighed.

"That still doesn't get us past men with machine guns." Turning, I leaned around the tree behind me and peeked at the top of the hill. "They look spaced within five feet of each other to you?"

"Yes, why? Can you make a shield again?" Alek asked.

"Maybe," I said, though I had something else in mind. I pulled on my magic, ignoring the dance of red spots at the corner of my vision and the sharp pain that did a jig between my eyes. I was tired, but I hadn't hit my limit. Not yet.

But I was tired of shields. Tired of bullets. There had to be another way. I looked around and fixated on Alek's shirt. He'd pulled on a white teeshirt from his house trailer and a black sweater over it. The teeshirt showed a little above the collar line of the sweater. I was sure Ezee would have been horrified.

"Give me your undershirt," I said to Alek, the stupidly crazy idea forming in my head growing more and more real by the second.

He pursed his lips but to his credit he pulled off his sweater, then his teeshirt, and handed it over, tugging his sweater back on. I picked up a dry stick from the ground and tied the shirt to it. Pulling my braid over my shoulder, I yanked out the tie and shook my hair down my back. I wanted to look unmistakably female and human before I walked out into the open.

"Wait for my signal," I said. "I'm going to try to get closer."

"They are going to shoot you," Alek said.

"Maybe," I said. "But those are human men up there. I know a thing or three about men."

"You are covered in blood."

I looked down. He had a point, but fuck it. "That might help sell the whole 'helpless and in need of saving by dicks.'"

"What's the signal?" Alek asked with a resigned look on his face.

"Them dying or me getting shot. Whichever happens first." I picked up my makeshift truce flag and grinned. I didn't give him a chance to respond, stumbling out of the tree line and into the grass, walking straight up the hill toward the men holding machine guns.

Behind me I heard Aurelio mutter something that sounded like "mates."

The men didn't shoot. I saw movement among them, and the murmur of voices filtered down to me as I walked, waving my flag.

"Don't shoot," I called up to them, pitching my voice higher than it normally was. "I need help!" I fake-stumbled and moved closer, letting my magic fill my veins, readying a spell in my mind. I knew what I wanted to do; it was just a matter of getting close enough, of connecting.

"Lady," one of the men yelled, sitting partially up. "This is a restricted area. Back down." He sounded distressed. I didn't know what Eva's instructions had been, but shooting unarmed women who looked already hurt and were asking for help clearly hadn't been covered.

Just a few feet closer. Closer. I labored up the hill, covering another ten feet. Then another. I could make out their eyes through their balaclavas. One of the men on the side dropped low over his gun, sighting down on me. The others still looked confused and unfocused, but I was running out of time.

Forty feet out, I threw the spell. Purple lightning arced from my outstretched hand, zapping into the man who had spoken. It hit him hard and threw him back before spreading between him and his companions, forking out to either side in a spectacular light show. I dropped flat to the hill, wincing as my injured leg twinged, and pressed my face to the still damp grass.

Silence. Then I heard Alek and Aurelio running up the hill behind me. I sat up and looked at the porch.

The mercenaries lay where the lighting had thrown them away from their guns. None of them were moving. I shoved away the pang of guilt about it. Alek was right— it did get easier. It helped, of course, that I was pretty sure they had been about to gun down an unarmed woman. Hard to feel guilty in the face of that little fact.

We climbed the remainder of the hill together.

"What did you do to them?" Aurelio asked me as Alek checked the bodies methodically for signs of life, stripping them of their weapons as he went.

"Chain lightning," I said. "When you absolutely, positively got to kill every last motherfucker in the room, accept no substitutes."

"You are very odd," the Bitterroot alpha said. He turned away from me with a frown and, putting his fingers into his mouth, whistled back at the woods.

"Guess you don't watch a lot of movies," I muttered. My badass references were wasted on this guy.

Wolves streamed up the hill behind Aurelio. He met the eyes of a leggy white wolf and nodded as though it were speaking to him.

"These are the only men with guns out here. Everyone else is inside," he said.

I looked up at the huge doors. "I think I can blast through these," I said. High on magic, I was pretty sure I could blast through anything at the moment. I was going to pay for this later.

"Or we could go in the side door," Alek said, pointing to a smaller door set near the corner of the hall, at the edge of the stone porch. "With the key Liam gave me before he died."

So much for a super-grand, dramatic entrance. Some guys just don't know how to have fun.

Aurelio agreed that he and his second, the white wolf, would come in with us, but that the rest of his pack would stay outside and guard our flanks. He actually said "guard our flanks." It was kind of adorable. I wished that Ezee had been here to hear it.

Alek unlocked the door, and we entered the great hall with him leading the way. I readied shields just in case there were more men with guns.

The side door led into a small foyer where a second door opened into the great hall proper. That door was also locked, but Alek's key opened it. The door opened inward and Alek poked his head around before nodding and walking through.

As soon as we passed through the door, I heard people talking, the sounds of a crowd washing over me like a tangible wave. The air inside was heavy and warm—the ceiling was far above and there was plenty of space even with hundreds of bodies inside, but the hall was still crowded enough to heat the air, to change it. The stone walls shimmered slightly and I recognized the kind of soundproof shielding that Alek sometimes used. Eva's doing.

The hallway we'd emerged into opened wide almost immediately to reveal a cavernous room. Benches lined the walls and there was a gallery level above, an iron spiral staircase on my left leading up to it. Men and women covered the benches, many sitting, and some standing above in the gallery. A large stone slab engraved with knotwork sat in the middle of the floor, raised a few inches from the stones around it. Wulf's final resting place, I guessed. A small group of shifters stood at the head of the slab, Eva among them.

The crowd's murmuring conversations turned to exclamations as we entered. Bodies moved aside, eyes questioning, as the four of us walked into the open center of the hall.

"The hall is sealed," Eva said, fear and anger clouding her face and making her look meaner and uglier than ever. "This is a place for wolves. You are not welcome here."

"Am I not?" Aurelio asked before Alek or I could respond. He looked around at the assembled alphas. "I am wolf. I am alpha. This woman once prevented me from pledging to Ulfr's Peace. I will not be turned away again." His eyes dropped to the elaborately carved stone. "He was my friend."

A shorter speech than he'd given Alek and I, but it worked. Murmurs of "Softpaw" and "Bitterroot alpha" rippled around the hall.

"The Peace? It does nothing for us. It has neutered us. We are wolves. We are alphas. Do not be stupid." Eva strode forward, spitting onto the stone.

Freyda stepped out of the group as well, following Eva, outrage in every line of her body.

"Eva Phillips," Alek called out before Freyda could speak. He raised a hand, his gesture and words commanding immediate silence. "You are a murderer and a liar. I am here to bring you to justice."

"Justice? You know nothing of what we were, cat. Once we were feared, respected. The Council gave us real power, ultimate authority. There was a time when they spoke to us directly instead of feeding us vague visions and unhappy dreams. I will be the alpha of alphas and there will be no Peace. Let the Council come and stop me."

"I am still Justice," Alek responded, moving forward with the stalking grace of a hunting cat.

Aurelio and I backed off. Freyda looked at Alek and she, too, moved backward, until just the two of them stood on opposite ends of the stone slab.

"So the Council sent you?" Eva mocked.

"No," Alek said.

From the soft exclamations all around me, I wasn't the only one surprised by this revelation.

"But," he continued, pulling his feather talisman out of his sweater and holding it so that the silver caught the dim light filtering in through the upper windows and glinted, "I am still a Justice. The scales will balance."

Eva's eyes widened, and she snarled at him, flicking her hand in a "now" gesture.

Movement and a soft cry from the upper gallery dragged my gaze away from Eva. I recognized the two green-eyed brothers from the parking lot by Liam's body the day before as they stood up in the gallery, machine guns in their hands. Every man and woman near them also pulled out a machine gun.

The hall had just become a barrel, and we were the fish.

Alek roared; the same deep coughing sound as earlier at the Henhouse reverberated throughout the hall. It was an impressive sound coming from a human throat, human lungs. Around me bodies turned from human to wolf, dropping from two legs to four, until I was standing at the edge of a sea of wolves. Beside me a huge black wolf with a wide white streak down his back crouched and growled, golden eyes focused above. Aurelio. I stepped in closer to him and looked up.

In the gallery, the men and women holding machine guns had stayed human as well. I squinted, making out earbuds and the lines of a cords running from their ears. No wonder Eva had gestured to signal them. One of the brothers held a gun that looked more like one of the paintball rifles we used. It made me nervous, though I didn't know why.

Eva was still human as well. She laughed. "Thank you. Saved me the trouble of forcing them to shift later."

Alek glared at her and snarled. "I challenge you, Eva. You want the old ways? Then let us fight, tooth and claw. We shall see who is right."

"You are a tiger," she said. "Hardly a fair fight."

"I am still weak from your poison," he said.

"Good point," she said. "That reminds me." She gestured again, pointing at Alek and making eye contact with the brother holding the air rifle.

"No," I yelled in warning as I threw my power at Alek, trying to shove him aside. I recognized the gun now. It was like the ones some of the scientists used when tagging wolves out in the River of No Return Wilderness. A tranq dart gun.

Only I knew it wouldn't hold a tranquilizer.

The dart stuck him in the shoulder instead of the neck as my magic shoved him sideways. With a snarl he ripped it out and threw it down, then shifted immediately and sprang at Eva.

She pulled a small cylinder from her pocket, gripping it in her hand before she shifted as well. She wasn't that big a human, but her wolf form was massive, thick with muscle and covered in sleek red fur.

Tiger-Alek dwarfed her, but his leap missed as she sprang sideways. Around the edges of the hall the wolves pressed backward against the walls, giving the two Justices room. One wolf tried to climb the stairs, snarling up at the shifters with guns. A gun cracked, impossibly loud in the hall, and the wolf fell back, screaming in pain.

Alek and Eva circled each other. He kept lunging and trying to grab her, but she was too quick, leaping out of reach and circling around, snapping at his legs and forcing him to twist and turn. She was waiting, I saw—waiting for him to weaken. My hands tightened into fists and I wanted to fry her where she stood. Alek's pale eyes caught mine, and I held back. He had made me promise that Eva was his. This wasn't my fight, unfair though it was.

I had to trust him. He had shifted before the poison had gotten deep into him. He could take her. I hoped.

Beside me, Aurelio moved away, stalking along the edge of the wolves, heading for the stairs. I hesitated for a moment, worried about Alek, but gave myself a mental shake and followed Aurelio, turning my attention to the gunmen above.

The brother with the dart gun noticed us moving, and nudged his brother. I hoped I was close enough and sent a bolt of lightning streaking into him. The lighting arced between them and blasted both brothers off their feet, smashing them back into their companions. My spell was weaker than the one I'd thrown at the men outside, the lightning dying out before traveling to more than the two of them. Fatigue turned my legs to lead and my head felt about ready to explode, but I threw another bolt into the gallery, then another, striking as many as I could.

The remainder started trying to shoot me, but automatic weapons aren't exactly accurate. I threw up a shield, trying to angle it so bullets would skip off at an upward angle, away from the wolves trying to back away from me.

"Get out," I yelled at them. "The side door, go." But no one was listening, their attention either on the gallery where Aurelio had gained the stairs, or on the tiger and wolf fighting in the center of the hall.

The alphas meant to see the fight through. Idiots.

Aurelio and his white wolf companion ripped into the gunmen above me, and I dared not throw more lightning around. The gunfire stopped as the few remaining found they had more pressing, and toothy, problems. It looked like Aurelio had things in hand as three more brave alphas flowed up the stairs and joined in subduing the last of the gunmen.

I staggered against a bench and sat heavily, trying to breathe through my exhaustion, my gaze returning to the fight. Wolves around me were turning back to men and women, taking up seats again. They all gave me wide berth, leaving me with a perfect front-row seat.

Blood ran down Alek's flank, staining his pristine white coat. There was blood on his mouth as well, and a wound gaped in Eva's right shoulder where his teeth had found purchase. She glanced up at the gallery and snarled. Alek took advantage of her distraction to spring, his tail whipping back and forth as he landed on her, pinning her partially beneath him. His jaw snapped closed just above where her head should have been as she shifted to human and then back to wolf in a blink, avoiding the killing blow. Her jaws sank into his foreleg, and he twisted, ripping into her injured shoulder again with his teeth. She rolled out from under him, fur and blood dripping from her mouth.

Alek didn't let her go far; his were teeth still locked in her shoulder. He tore free a huge chunk of fur and flesh, revealing the white of her bone before a curtain of blood covered it. So much blood, spurting from severed arteries. She was too hurt to continue. She had to be. I leaned forward, holding my breath, waiting for Alek to deliver the killing blow.

Eva screamed, scrabbling away from him. She couldn't stand, however, instead crouching low on the stone slab, her blood gushing down and slowly painting the knotwork engravings crimson. She became human again, her hand still clutching whatever she had pulled from her pocket before the fight.

Alek shifted back to human as well. His face was gaunt, his eyes filled with rage and pain.

"It is over," he said. "I find you guilty of murder, Eva Phillips. I find you unworthy to wear the mark of the Justice."

She laughed, her eyes darting around crazily. "It's a stupid charm I bought from a stand on the road," she said. "My feather melted away like ice in sunlight the night I killed that stupid wolf bitch. The Council has already turned on me. But the Peace will never succeed, even if I die. The Council is sick. This way of life is over. We will find a new way."

"I am here. The Council is here through me," Alek said. "It does not matter. You will die by my hand." He walked toward her cautiously, not trusting her. I applauded that.

"No," she said, spitting blood. "You'll all die by mine." And she raised her hand, revealing the silvery object. It looked like a pen, but with a button on top.

I'd watched enough action movies to recognize that. A switch.

"I had Wulf buried with a little something extra," she said, still cackling as blood frothed from her mouth.

I didn't stop to think, to breathe. I hardly knew I was moving, only that I wouldn't make it to her in time. Grabbing my d20 talisman with both hands, I threw my magic out and anchored it like a tether to the bloody stone beneath Eva's body. Then I pulled. The tether yanked me forward and I went flying across the floor and slammed into Eva as she pushed down on the button.

"Get out get them out go go please go," I was screaming as I threw my arms around her, wrapping my magic all around us and the stone, pouring every ounce of myself into the shield.

I couldn't see if Alek obeyed before the world exploded.

There was pain, but it was the kind of pain that because abstract very quickly. Like being cut deep with a very sharp blade. The ache is there and intense, but it doesn't feel real. The cut looks like it has happened to someone else and your body tries to tell you that this isn't your limb, that isn't your wound.

This won't kill me. But it felt like dying. My eardrums exploded, my head ringing like a million bells. Darkness threatened, but I fought it back with my power, pushing against unconsciousness, embracing the blinding pain. I couldn't feel Eva in my arms anymore. I wasn't convinced I still had arms. My world became a thought, narrowed down to a single desire.

So much pressure. White hot, molten, bubbling up against me like lava. My shields strained, the power in me waning, drained too far.

Keep the shield up. No more family, no more friends are going to die because of a bomb. Ever. Not if I still live to stop them. Never. Again.

Something inside me broke loose. Like a joint popping back into alignment that I hadn't known was out until it set itself again.

The lava turned to warmth. The pain disappeared. I floated in a sea of power, breathing in it, channeling it into the shield as though I had the universe itself at my fingertips. I breathed in flame, inhaled the pressure of the explosion, and breathed out magic, pure, unfamiliar power that was both mine and not mine.

If this is death, I thought, *I don't mind it so much.*

"Not death," said a gentle, masculine voice in my head. "But you aren't ready yet. Go back to sleep."

And then the power slipped away and the warmth faded back into heat.

There was something hard and smooth as glass beneath my body. My head pounded like a motherfucker. For a long second I just breathed, amazed that I could, afraid to move in case the blinding pain returned. I tested by wiggling my big toe.

It was there and intact. I felt it scrape against the smooth surface beneath me. My hands were underneath me, my talisman pressing against my palm. I opened my eyes and blinked a few times, trying to figure out where I was. Glassy red stone curved upward from in front of my face, as though I lay in a steep bowl. I rolled onto my back and my foot hit something that clattered on the glass as it moved.

Above me the roof of the great hall looked intact. I moved my eyes as Alek appeared at the lip of the giant bowl I lay in.

"Jade?" he said, his voice and face filled with disbelief and then joy. He slid down beside me as I sat up.

"I'm okay," I said. My voice sounded like I had smoked a few too many packs of cigarettes and I coughed, trying to clear my dry throat. A memory of breathing in fire, of bathing in flames and having more power than a god flickered through my mind, slippery and unreal. I pushed it away and looked around.

There was no sign of Eva. At my feet was Samir's dagger. It had survived the blast, which didn't surprise me. My clothes, not so much. I sat in a depression in the stone floor about eight feet across and three or so feet deep. The stone was blood red and melted smooth like glass. Alek crouched down beside me, but didn't touch me.

I climbed slowly to my feet, taking the hand he offered. Other than being totally naked, I felt fine. My body looked fine—not a burn mark or wound on me. My hair fell over my shoulders, waist-length and glossy, as though I'd washed and combed it recently. I reached up and felt for the shorter bit where Haruki had shot off part of my hair, but that was gone. Twisting my leg, I looked at the back of my thigh. No sign of that wound, either.

"Huh," I said, bending and picking up Samir's knife.

The hall was empty, the great doors thrown wide open. Beyond I saw shifters milling around. Aurelio and

Freyda stood side by side on the porch, just outside the doorway, talking with their heads together.

I took a deep breath. "So, that's over, I guess." I tried on a smile and looked at Alek.

"No," he said. "But our part is, I think."

I tried to climb up out of the bowl, and slipped. Alek's arms came around me and he lifted me up. Fucking hell. Not again.

"Put me down," I demanded as he jumped easily out of the bowl.

"You can barely stand," he said.

"But I *can* stand," I said. "This happens, like, every fucking time. I pull off big magic, knock myself on my ass, and then you show up and carry me home. Fuck that. This time I am walking out of here on my own two feet."

His lips twitched and the concern in his eyes turned to humor. He set me down, keeping a steadying hand on my elbow.

"Would you like a shirt, Lady Godiva?" he asked, his smile turning into a smirk.

I looked out at the gathered crowd and then down at my naked body. My hair was doing a Godiva thing, covering my breasts if not much else. It was definitely a sign of my exhaustion that I had forgotten in the last twenty seconds that I was sporting the emperor's latest wardrobe malfunction.

"Yes," I muttered. "Shirt might be good."

He gave me his sweater. I pulled it on and it covered me nearly to my knees, the sleeves falling over my hands. I rolled them up and picked up Samir's knife again. Good enough. I turned to Alek and gently touched the purple and black bruises on his arm and shoulder.

"You okay?" I said, looking up at him.

"I will live," he promised me, bending to kiss my nose.

"All right," I said. Squaring my shoulders and trying not to lean on his offered arm too heavily, I walked out of the hall on my own two damn feet.

I passed out cold about thirty seconds later, but that's besides the point.

Freyda became the new alpha of alphas, Alek told us later. Aurelio and many others pledged their blood to Wulf's sword, but some of the alphas left without pledging and there was still a great deal of suspicion around who had sided with Eva or not.

It seemed the future of the Peace was still in the air.

Eva was dead, assumed vaporized in the explosion. Wulf's body was now sealed beneath the depression I'd created with my power, though I guessed it had been vaporized as well.

I told my friends my version of events, leaving out the weird experience in the middle of the explosion. I didn't know what to think of it. My power felt normal after a day of sleeping and eating vast quantities of Rosie's

French toast. No strange warmth, no sudden desire to inhale flames.

Haruki's memories lurked in my mind, his knowledge waiting for examination, but I had had enough of fire for a while and left them there. I left my shop closed for a few days, too, choosing to stay at the Henhouse.

I pretended it was because I needed to recover and make sure all my friends were healed, but the truth was, I was afraid to resume my life, afraid of what might happen now that people knew what I really was. I didn't believe for a moment that what had happened at the Den would stay quiet among the supernatural residents of Wylde.

It was Harper, as usual, who made me go home and return to work. Harper who nagged me into resuming my normal life.

My shop felt musty, but aired out after we propped the door open for a while. It was Thursday morning and nobody came in, which wasn't unusual. The college would open for classes in just over a week, so I figured business would pick up then. I didn't mind the quiet.

Harper was camped out in her chair, playing *Hearthstone* and swearing at the RNG gods. I sat up on my stool, a full box of unopened *Magic: The Gathering* booster packs in front of me, debating if I should just open them and sell the individual cards to keep the packs intact. I kind of wanted the mindless work of sorting them, and the little bits of happy discovery that came from each opened pack as I looked to see what the mythic or rare card was.

"Shouldn't you have the blinds down, just in case that assassin comes back?" Harper asked, glancing at the front windows and open door.

"He's not coming back," I said. I'd neglected to tell my friends about Haruki and how it had ended. There had been too many other things to say, and the moment had passed. No one had asked about the assassin all week, either.

"Wait, you sound really sure."

"You could say I'm dead sure," I said, giving her a grim smile.

"Okay, back up, when did that happen?" Harper slapped her laptop closed and sat up straighter.

I sighed and told her the full story. Or almost anyway. I tried to leave out the part at the end.

"You stopped off on Sunday morning and had a ninja battle? And you seriously didn't think it was worth telling me about?" She shook her head at me. "Crazy lady."

"I killed a man," I said softly. "I didn't really want to talk about it."

"He's not the first man you've killed," Harper said with a shrug.

I flinched. "I more than killed him," I told her.

Understanding dawned on her face, and she took a deep breath. "Good. You need more power to stop Samir, right? Why not use the tools you are given?"

"This doesn't remotely bother you, does it?" I searched her face but she only looked back at me with open, honest eyes.

"Some people need killing," she said.

"Easy for someone who has never killed to say."

Harper went very still and then shrugged far too casually.

"What?" I said. "Azalea! Who did you kill? When?"

"Someone who needed killing," she said. "You want the story, I want cake." She pointed at the door.

"Cupcakes okay?" I said, taking pity on her. She looked profoundly uncomfortable, and I understood the feeling. Talking about murder wasn't a comfortable thing.

"Lemon, please," she said, relaxing a little.

I grabbed my wallet and walked next door to Brie's Bakery. The nice weather was holding and the morning sun sparkled off the display cases. The bakery smelled amazing as always. It was too late in the morning for the coffee and paper crowd and too early for the lunch crowd, so I almost had the place to myself, and there was no line. Two regulars sat at a table in the corner far from the door by the window, playing checkers and eating fruit tarts.

I walked up to the front and contemplated the cupcake selection while Brie finished loading a fresh tray of Danishes onto a shelf. There was lemon today, but I wanted chocolate. Or vanilla. One of each? Oh, the difficult choices in front of me.

"Hey, Brie," I said when she turned around. "Two lemon and two vanilla with chocolate frosting." I pointed at the cupcakes.

"No," she said.

I straightened up and looked at her. Her normally cheerful face was cold and hard, all warmth missing from her eyes. Shit.

"No?" I asked, confused.

"You are not welcome here," she said. Her eyes flickered to the two customers at the table and she lowered her voice, adding, "Sorceress."

My confusion melted away into unhappy anger.

"I'm the same person I was yesterday, or last week. Or these last five years," I said.

"I will not clasp a snake to my breast," she responded. "Now leave. You are banned from this place."

A snake? What? I backed away. "Brie," I said, trying to think of words that would help, that would stop the hatred pouring off her. The air crackled with magic, her usual warm, healing power turning bitter and sharp to my senses.

"Do not make me call the sheriff and have you arrested for trespassing," she said.

The two regulars stopped their game and looked up at us with wide eyes. We were starting to make a scene. I realized there was nothing I could say or do that wouldn't just make things worse, so I turned and left.

I walked the dozen steps back to my shop in a daze. The door chimed as I entered and Harper looked up.

"No cupcakes?" she asked, seeing my empty hands.

"The cupcakes were a lie," I said, trying to joke through the tears that threatened.

"Jade," she said, not fooled for a moment. "What happened?"

"Word is out," I said. "As I knew it would be. Small town. Brie banned me for being a sorceress. She's afraid of me now."

"But you've lived right next to her for, like, half a decade."

"She called me a snake," I said. "Like I was just waiting to bite."

"She's an idiot. I am never eating her pastries again. Ever. And neither will the twins or my mom or anyone else I know, once I tell them about this."

"Harper, that isn't necessary. Sorcerers don't have the best reps, you know that. She can't be sure I'm not a danger to her." Her fierce protectiveness made me smile and pushed down the sadness inside.

"Fuck that. I bet that is all Samir's fault anyway. You don't deserve this shit." She got up and wrapped me into a bony hug.

"Thanks, furball," I said, hugging her back. It was good to have friends.

I sent Harper to get sandwiches an hour later, not quite ready to go back outside. I was pretty sure the sandwich guys at Pete's Deli were human, but better safe than hungry.

I was in the back part of the store, dusting off the painted display miniatures when my door chimed and my wards hummed, warning me of magic. The scent of cloves preceded the woman into my shop. I walked to the counter where she waited, recognizing the head librarian. I couldn't recall her name, however. It started with a P, I thought. She was middle-aged, with brown hair laced with grey pulled up into a tidy bun. She had on jeans and a teeshirt that read "Books are Grrrreat" over the picture of a goofy-looking tiger.

"Afternoon," I said, though I had the feeling from the sharp scent of her magic that this wasn't a social call or her wanting games or comics for the library.

"I'll make this brief," she said, wrinkling her pale nose as though my shop smelled like dirty laundry. "You are not welcome in this town, sorceress. I require you to leave as soon as possible."

"Um, no?" I said, standing up very straight. I resisted the urge to summon my magic and push back on the power she had clearly readied and brought with her. A protective spell, I was guessing. I was willing to bet it was no match for what I could throw at her. But petty escalation wasn't going to help my new PR issue. "I've lived here in peace for five years. I'm a business owner."

I didn't mention I actually owned the whole building, including the bakery next door and Ciaran's Curios. Both Ciaran and Brie leased from me, though neither knew it. I'd bought the building through one of my fake names and figured I'd let that part stay a secret.

"We allowed you to stay because we thought you were just a young witch. You did not bother to introduce yourself to the coven, but we considered that ignorance on your part, not secrecy."

"Coven?" I said. "I had no idea there was a coven." That meant there were at least twelve others. Great.

"We are more powerful than you might believe," she said, folding her arms across her chest. "Do not think you can come after us. Our power will never be yours."

"I don't want your power, I have my own, thanks." I dropped all pretense of politeness and glared at her. "I'm staying right here. Live with it."

"You have thirty days to leave. After that, we will make life very, very unpleasant for you," she said, her mouth pressing into a tight pink line.

"Oh for fuck's sake," I said. "Are you seriously threatening me?"

"Thirty days," she repeated. "Or else…"

I started to ask her "Or else what?" but was interrupted by Ciaran.

The leprechaun who had been my friend and neighbor for half a decade filled the doorway of my shop and clapped his hands together sharply, drawing both my and the witch's attention.

"Peggy Victoria Olsen," he said in a booming voice that was completely at odds with his short, stout stature. "You will not threaten my friend. Leave. Now."

"Ciaran, do you know what this woman is?"

"She is my friend," he said. "You have no power here, Peggy. No authority. Go. I am not so much a gentleman that I won't make you leave by force if I must."

Peggy the witch librarian sniffed loudly and turned on her heels. She stomped past Ciaran, who moved aside just enough to let her pass.

I wanted to hug him, but settled for thanking him profusely in Irish.

"Think nothing of it," he said, accepting the offer of a seat in Harper's chair. "I do not care what you are. Only who."

I narrowed my eyes. "You've known this whole time, haven't you?"

He winked at me and tugged on a springy red curl near one of his oversized ears.

"It's a poor leprechaun I'd be if I couldn't keep a secret or three," he said. "Ah, there is Miss Azalea with your lunch, I think." He stood up. "You are welcome for tea anytime, Jade Crow."

"As are you, Ciaran Hayes," I said formally, offering my hands.

He took them and squeezed briefly. Then, exchanging a greeting with Harper, he breezed back out my door with the same energy he'd entered. I felt a deep relief that he was still on my side.

"What'd Ciaran want? Don't tell me he's banning you, too?" Harper said as she put the bag of sandwiches down on the counter.

"No, he's still my friend. The librarian, on the other hand…" I sighed.

"Mrs. Olsen? What did she want?"

"She's a witch," I said. "And she's given me thirty days to leave town. *Or else.*" And with that I collapsed into giggles, because it was better than crying or screaming.

After staying at the Henhouse for a few nights, it felt strange to be alone in my apartment again. I took a long bath and then put on a season of *Clone Wars*. I needed something fun to distract me from the events of the day. At least no one else had come in and threatened me or banned me from their business.

I picked up the folded copy of the *Wylde Gazette* I'd grabbed from the counter in the store where Harper had abandoned it. The front-page article was about the Lansings. They had been reported missing on Tuesday by Jed's sister. Last night they had been found, following a huge search effort. Their car had apparently gone off the road and caught fire in one of the more twisty parts between here and Bear Lake. The bodies had been so burned that the cops refused to confirm it was the Lansings, but the VIN on the car matched, so the paper was comfortable reporting it.

I didn't know how Alek had managed that one, but I guessed it gave the family closure while still protecting the shifters. Balance again. I sighed and tossed the paper into the recycling.

I heard the creak of someone coming up my back stairs and paused by the kitchen door. A light tap followed, and I opened the door.

Alek stood there with a bag of Chinese in his hand and a gentle smile on his face.

"You are getting sloppy," I said. "I heard you coming up the stairs."

He shrugged. "I made noise on purpose."

"Sure you did. That lo mein?"

We settled down on my couch with chopsticks and passed the boxes back and forth, just eating and sharing company for a while. After my belly was full of noodles and spicy chicken, I told him about my day.

"It will be more difficult for you here now," he said with a sigh. "But you will stay?"

"Of course," I said. "I'm sort of in for the penny and the pound at this point. I am done running away from my problems. From now on I run at my problems, preferably armed to the teeth."

"Good," he said.

"What about you?"

"Me?"

"Yes," I said. I set down my chopsticks and curled up on the couch beside him, tucking my feet under his thigh. "The Council didn't send you back here. You told Eva that."

"No. I came back because I missed you. Missed this." He waved a hand around, gesturing at the apartment, at the food, at me. "I ran into Henry at a gas station outside town. He was searching for his mate and recognized me. He thought I was here to help him, and I let him believe that."

"You totally lied," I said, smiling to take some of the bite out of my words.

Alek ducked his head and took a deep breath. "Yes. I maintain that you are a bad influence." That thought seemed to sober him further and he looked at me, searching my face. "Before, when I left? It was because the Council sent me away."

"To help somewhere else, to work a case, right?" I reached out and tucked a stray lock of hair behind his ear.

He pressed his cheek into my palm. "Yes, and no. They warned me to stay away from you. They do not want me here."

I looked into his ice-blue eyes and saw shadows lurking there. "What else?" I asked, because I knew there was more he wasn't saying.

"They showed me my death," he said, his voice dropping almost to a whisper, a growl. "They showed me that if I stayed here, I would die."

"I don't fucking accept that," I said, curling my fingers into a fist and pulling my hand back. "They didn't warn you about Eva. They didn't send anyone to stop what happened here. I'm sorry, Alek, but I am beginning to seriously doubt this Council of yours."

I had watched him dying beside me, had felt the poison burning away his heart. No way was I ever going to let anything happen to him. Never. Fuck the Council and their stupid visions. I was a sorceress. I would change the future, make it mine.

"I am, as well," he said so quietly I thought I'd imagined the words. He wrapped his hands around mine, warming me. "I still sense them. I still have my gifts, my talisman. I do not know what their plan is. But I will stay here. That is not negotiable anymore."

"Good," I said. "Because we have some serious talking to do."

"We do?" He raised an eyebrow at me. "Should I be nervous?"

"No, but I want to know you, Alek. I mean, I don't even know if you have a family, siblings. Where you grew up. Anything. You've at least met my family."

"You never asked," he said. "And I only met your family because someone tried to kill them and they came asking for help. You didn't exactly share their existence or that you'd been born to shifters before that."

Touché. Another point for Alek.

"All right, so both of us need to be better about this whole actually sharing thing." I made a face at him.

He dragged me into his lap and tucked my head under his chin. I curled against his impossible warmth, relaxing into him.

"I was born in Siberia," he said, his voice rumbling and making his chest vibrate against my cheek. "In the Irkutsk Oblast."

"Gesundheit," I said.

"Hush, kitten. If you want others to talk, you first must be silent."

I leaned up and nipped his chin. "Go on. Siblings?"

"I have two siblings. A brother and a sister."

"Let me guess, you are the oldest?" He seemed like an oldest, with his overdeveloped sense of responsibility.

"Technically, I suppose. By a minute or so."

"Wait," I said, sitting up and twisting in his lap so I could look at him. "You are a triplet? That's like crazy rare, right?"

"Yes, well, Mother was an overachiever." His eyes were unfocused, looking at memories far away and long ago. I remembered then that he was over sixty years old.

"Was? She's dead?"

"She died giving birth to us. Hemorrhaged, but she refused to shift with us inside her—she was convinced it would kill us. By the time they cut us out, it was too late."

Oh. I laid my head back down on his chest. "Are you close to your siblings? Did your father raise you?"

"We are tigers. I do not even know who my father was." I felt him shrug. "We were raised by my grandmother. She lives still, in Russia. It has been a long time since I spoke with her, or my siblings."

"When did you become a Justice?"

"I was sixteen when I was called, chosen. Carlos, who you met at Three Feathers, came to me not long after and took me away to the States for training."

"And you've never been back?"

"I have. But it was not the same."

I understood that, too. "Thank you for telling me," I said.

"Anything," he murmured into my hair.

Anything? I decided to test that. I sat back up.

"When Eva triggered the bomb, did you see anything?" I recalled his face as he looked down at me, the awe there. I had caught hints of that awe in him, speculative glances in the days after.

He looked away from me, staring into the middle distance again. Then shook his head. "I do not know. There was much chaos, people trying to leave, getting the doors open. Your magic shoved me away from you. Then there was a bubble of light, and inside…" He shook his head again. "I think I know what I thought I saw. But it is impossible. And the memory is unclear; it won't stay for me to look at it."

"As though it's something you knew but have forgotten and now can only remember that you have forgotten, but not what you forgot," I said.

"That almost made sense," he said, smiling. "But yes, it is slippery like that."

"What do you think you saw?" I asked.

"A dragon," he said softly.

"Oh." I searched my own memory. The heat, the light, that lingering sense of wonder and power. No dragons.

Alek pulled me tight against him and kissed my forehead. "I told you it was crazy."

"Crazy is my new middle name." I nuzzled his neck, glad to be held. Glad he was whole and safe.

"While we are on the subject of crazy things," he said.

"Go on." I licked his throat. He even tasted like vanilla. I probably tasted like soy sauce.

"I love you, Jade Crow," he said.

I froze, my mind going blank for a moment. I struggled to form the perfect response, to find the words to tell him how much hearing that meant to me, how my life was better with him in it, how I wanted to give us a real chance, to make this relationship work and let our past be damned. I hesitated too long, unable to find the right words to begin, and the moment stretched out and became awkward.

So I settled for a Star Wars reference instead.

"I know," I said, burying my head in his shoulder.

And somehow, with those two words, he heard all the things I had meant to say.

Tess watched Samir from the corner of her eye as he spoke quietly into his cell phone. Tension built in his broad shoulders and his golden eyes flared with power as he snapped the phone shut and turned away from the huge picture window that overlooked the valley below his mansion.

"The assassin has failed," he said.

"I told Tess it wouldn't work," Clyde said in his nasal, whining voice.

Tess vowed, again, to rip out his vocal cords before she killed the little bastard. But Clyde was still Samir's apprentice, sharing her station in life like a sibling. Samir expected them to get along. So she could go on pretending.

She was faking the rest of her life—why not this little thing, too?

"It was diverting," Samir said. "But now it is Clyde's choice."

Tess knew what Clyde would choose. She looked over to where he sat, resting like a fat and pampered lap dog on the white leather sofa. His blonde hair was artfully messy, his silk shirt unbuttoned just enough to show off the smooth muscles of his chest. He was slight but kept himself in excellent shape. Samir preferred his lovers to be in shape. He required beauty in all things around him.

"I want to go," Clyde said. "Enough fooling around. Let me bring you her heart myself."

Jade Crow. Samir's obsession. It grated on Clyde. He hated that Samir cared more for a woman who had left him years ago than for the man who lived with him now, fawning after his every whim.

Clyde did not understand Samir. He was young, and he did not see the danger in a life lived too long yet. Boredom was a terrible burden, and Samir was easily bored.

Soon, Tess knew, Samir would grow tired of Clyde. Then the young sorcerer would become another heart for the reaping.

Tess did her best to never be boring. A delayed execution was better than nothing.

She looked at Samir, drinking in his aquiline, dark features, and his masculine beauty. She focused on her attraction to him, pushing down her revulsion, her fear, shoving it aside.

"I wish to go as well," she said. She lifted a thin shoulder as though to say "why not?" To convey to him that she merely wanted in on the fun, that this wasn't an important request either way. If she showed it was important, he might refuse her out of spite. Or start asking her questions that wouldn't be safe to answer.

"I don't need her," Clyde said, staring daggers at Tess.

She smiled blandly at him. "Of course not, dear."

"Enough, both of you." Samir chuckled and shook his head, his expression benevolent and amused, but his golden eyes sharp. "You will both go. Bring me Jade's heart. I will make a new container tonight. I will be watching closely. Do not fail me."

"What about her friends?" Clyde asked. "That big blond guy?"

"Do with them whatever you like," Samir said.

Clyde's smile made Tess's skin try to crawl off her bones. She bit the inside of her lip and kept her feelings off her face. Clyde's expertise was in raising demons, in perverting spirits of nature. He reveled in cruelty in ways that surprised even Samir on occasion.

Which was probably why Samir let him live. For now.

Tess's talents were subtler. She would find a way to make Clyde's rapid bull-in-a-china-shop methods mesh with her own. She smiled at Samir and inclined her head. "We will not fail you," she said.

Turning away before her face could betray her thoughts, she left the study. Only when she was safely behind her own wards, in her own room, did she relax.

Jade Crow had escaped Samir, not once, but twice. She had thwarted his attempts to find her for many years. And now she was visible again, surrounded by magic and inhuman friends. She had killed the assassin Tess had suggested they send after her. Tess had known that Samir wouldn't mind fattening Jade up a little more. Just as she knew he half expected his errant former protégé to kill both his apprentices.

Their lives meant nothing to Samir.

But Jade's life. Her life might mean something to Tess. Win or die, Tess was certain that the beautiful Native American sorceress held the key to Samir's death.

And that was something Tess was very interested in indeed.

If you want to be notified when Annie Bellet's next novel or collection is released, please sign up for the mailing list by going to: http://tinyurl.com/anniebellet. Your email address will never be shared and you can unsubscribe at any time. Want to find more Twenty-Sided Sorceress books? Go here http://overactive.wordpress.com/twenty-sided-sorceress/ for links and more information.

Word-of-mouth and reviews are vital for any author to succeed. If you enjoyed the book, please tell your friends and consider leaving a review wherever you purchased it.

Available December 9th, 2014
Pre-order Now

Also by Annie Bellet:

The Gryphonpike Chronicles:
Witch Hunt
Twice Drowned Dragon
A Stone's Throw
Dead of Knight
The Barrows (Omnibus Vol. 1)

Chwedl Duology:
A Heart in Sun and Shadow
The Raven King

Pyrrh Considerable Crimes Division Series:
Avarice

Short Story Collections:
The Spacer's Blade and Other Stories
River Daughter and Other Stories
Deep Black Beyond
Till Human Voices Wake Us
Dusk and Shiver
Forgotten Tigers and Other Stories

About the Author:

Annie Bellet lives and writes in the Pacific NW. She is the author of the *Gryphonpike Chronicles* and the *Twenty-Sided Sorceress* series, and her short stories have appeared in over two dozen magazines and anthologies. Follow her on her blog at "A Little Imagination".

http://overactive.wordpress.com/

CPSIA information can be obtained at www.ICGtesting.com
Printed in the USA
LVOW10s1713270815

451790LV00007B/805/P